Jason Summers

THE LOST BOY

By Jason Summers

For my third little girl, who is due any day now…

Chapter One

The cheers of the crowd and the roar of the loudspeakers were deafening. The bull rider stood on the highest section of the gate, watching the enormous beast underneath him vibrate and then crash again and again against the tall black gate in front of him. Beside him, the man in charge of opening the gate wore a black Akubra cowboy hat, worn and weathered with age, and watched the young bull rider with anticipation.

It was the rider's third and last ride of the night. The first one had been quick, thrown off as the gate opened, but the second had been more fruitful. A vicious and wild eleven second dance, as the amber-red sun cast its last rays of light across the wide arena. The crowd had cheered and screamed his name: Bryce, Bryce, Bryce! He was why they were there; to watch the best. And this last time he was going to get that big score again and show all the men watching from the cattle yard behind him why they should put some respect on his name.

A woman in the crowd watched on, waiting for the rider to explode out of the gate. Coming to the rodeo had been an annual tradition with her mother and father when she was a kid. The Gabinda Rodeo was one of the biggest in the state and attracted people from all the surrounding regions for the one day and night. It was the biggest event on the town's calendar and just because she didn't speak with her family anymore didn't mean that she wasn't going to create her own traditions with her partner and son.

She looked past her partner to the empty seat beside him as she waited for the rider to come out of the gate. She asked her partner, 'Have you seen Matty?'

Her partner kept his eyes down on the arena. 'Went to get an ice cream.'

She looked down at her phone; it had been a while. The announcer spoke again, bringing her attention back to the arena. 'Bryce Young is up next and has drawn a short straw in my opinion, he'll be riding one of the meanest buggers of the night, Bandsaw, a relative of one of Australia's most famous bulls, Chainsaw.'

Down in the chute she could see the young rider ready and waiting to mount the giant black bull. She had her own childhood memories of watching Chainsaw, one of the meanest bulls on the circuit in the 90s. After he'd buck off his next unsuspecting victim, he would trot off in a victorious lap around the arena with his head held high, like he was proud of what he had done. Her father had cheered and hollered back then just as the crowd had on this night at his offspring.

The volume of the crowd dropped for the shortest of moments as the anticipation built. Suddenly, she heard them yell 'Pull!' and the gateman unhitched the pin as the gate flew outwards to the crowd's roar. The rider was apparently turning some heads. Until recently, he was an unheard of farmworker who had exploded onto the scene earlier in the year with some daring rides. She was no expert by any means, but she had watched on in awe at his ride earlier in the day and at the grace with which he followed the aggressive movements of the giant animal underneath him. This time was no different, the bull shot out of the gate like a cannon, jumping in the air and spinning at the same time while the rider held on for dear life. The crowd screamed and cheered, and the announcer did his best to keep up with the action.

Time seemed to slow as she watched the young man being launched into the air again and again, but just as she thought he'd be nearing the eight second time limit where scoring began, something terrible happened. The bull turned violently and jumped, and as the rider's body fell forward towards the bull's neck, his chin collided directly with the point of the bull's horn all in one sickening motion. She knew in the moment it happened that it was serious because his body softened and rolled off the bull into a crumpled heap. She could hear the collective shriek of horror and then the screams of a woman in the crowd over the sound of anything else. 'Somebody help him!'

A woman behind her stood up quickly and yelled directly at her. 'Gabby, you said you were a nurse, didn't you?'

It was almost the truth. 'Yeah,' she lied.

The woman had already set off walking away. 'Come on, let's see if we can help him!'

She turned back to her partner. 'Can you please go and get Matty?'

Not fully convinced he was going to do the job asked of him, she had no choice but to follow the woman in front of her. The people in their row moved their legs to the side to allow for the two women to run along the stands and get to the tight metal staircase leading down to the fence. She followed the woman in front of her and could hear nothing but her own footsteps as a deathly pall was cast over the crowd. As she reached the fence, she could see two of the rodeo clowns carrying out a piece of corflute signage to shield the body that was on the dirt, so she knew it was serious.

'Gabby, this way,' came a voice from beside her.

A friend of her father's pointed her and the other woman in the direction of a gate in the fence line. He reached down and undid the slide locks on the top and bottom and pushed it inwards to allow the two women to access the arena. Checking to make sure the bull was now locked up, she ran across the brightly lit arena, suddenly feeling way out of her depth. She knew events like these were meant to have medical teams, but where were they? The parking spot for the ambulance was empty from where she could see.

The woman in front of her stopped beside the clowns and pointed back to her. 'She's a nurse, she can help.'

'Wait, I–'

One of the clowns cut her off, 'Thank God.' He moved to the left to allow them through. 'Help him. Please.'

She walked past the men and onward to the grisly scene. Three cowboys were all set around him. One was on his knees close to his head and the other two were on bended knee. One of the men on his knees looked up at the arrival and parroted the clowns. 'Can you help him?'

He stepped out of the way and Gabby got a good look at the rider for the first time. The horn had entered his chin and cast a violent path upwards through his mouth and behind his nose. She had expected to see a hardened and rough looking cowboy but the person on the ground was a boy, he seemed not much older than her own son. He was only just beginning to sprout facial hair from what she could see. 'Flip him on his side,' she said to the men. She was surprised at how quickly her limited medical training kicked in.

'Recovery position,' the woman said from behind her.

She kneeled down and pulled her jumper from around her waist and placed it under his head. He was still conscious, barely, and blood was dripping slowly from his nostrils, and more steadily out his mouth. 'You're going to be okay,' she said to the man, although she wasn't entirely sure that was the case. 'What's your name?'

'Bryce,' the man spluttered out. It was a good sign she thought, clearly the horn hadn't reached or hit anything near the brain or affected his memory.

'Bryce, my name is Gabby. We've called an ambulance and help is on its way.' She could hear the sirens in the distance as the other woman placed a dusty denim jacket over the man.

She felt her phone vibrating in her pocket and tried to look up into the silent crowd at the spot where her partner and son had been sitting, but the crowd had mostly dispersed. On towards the showgrounds and other festivities she guessed; the rodeo already a distant memory. As the sound of the sirens reached their crescendo, she spotted the red and blue flashing lights entering the dirt road that led to the cattle yards. The other woman that had directed her in the crowd had walked off with one of the cowboys to direct the ambulance where to enter.

Bryce coughed and whispered, the words coming out slowly between the gurgling of the blood still coming from his mouth: 'Did I get past eight seconds?'

The man across from Gabby grinned and patted him gently on the shoulder. 'You got it, mate, you did bloody good.'

The ambulance pulled up beside the small group, blocking the remaining crowd from witnessing any more gore and the two emergency services workers jumped out quickly. One of them, a man who looked no older than the young bull rider on the ground visibly gulped as he looked down at Bryce on the ground. Gabby and the other men all shuffled back slowly as the paramedics set to work stabilising Bryce for transport. Gabby stood up and turned back to the crowd, once again on the lookout for her partner. She finally remembered her phone and pulled it out of her jeans pocket and was shocked to see she had four missed calls.

'Everything okay?' asked the woman who had directed the ambulance. Before she could reply, she heard, 'Gabby! Gabby!' being yelled out from back near the fence line.

Gabby thought back to that moment later on, and realised it was that exact point in time when her mother's intuition kicked in. Something wasn't right. She could feel it. Deep in her stomach. She ran towards the fence as the woman followed.

Her partner Cameron was still behind the fence line, and ran towards the opening in the fence that she had entered the arena from. He looked frantic. He was sweating and had red dirt on his face; his hair was a mess. He bent over and had his hands on his knees, trying to catch his breath.

'What is it?' Gabby asked. 'Is it Matty? Where is he?'

Cameron, between gulping breaths, said, 'I've looked everywhere. I went to the hotdog stand; they haven't seen him. The rides. I saw Katherine Jones. I asked her. Nothing. I went to the public toilets. No-one. Nothing.'

Gabby was struggling to understand his frantic tone. 'What are you saying, Cam?'

Cameron finally calmed enough to speak clearly. 'Gabby. I can't find him anywhere. He's gone.'

Chapter Two

The state freeway system from the beginning of her journey was long gone, and the narrow country highway she now travelled along felt no different to the hundreds of others she had traversed over the last two years.

The landscape that sprawled out each side of the car was flat, brown and open. Dense thickets of bush were dotted along various sections of farmland as she headed further away from Sydney into the unknown.

Detective Joanna Gray was on leave. It was something that she wasn't used to, and didn't want to get used to. A week earlier, she had sat in her new apartment in the big city. A big city she never thought she would ever travel to, let alone live in. She felt like she was in an alien world. Her boss had given her two weeks off and then told her he would call her the following Friday to discuss the next steps. There was still an internal investigation going on in the background, due to her and her partner's actions in the mountain town of Blarnie a month ago, and she still wasn't sure what was going to come of it. It didn't really matter to her in the end. She knew what she had done was right.

The reason for her imposed leave, she guessed, was probably from the comments she had made during the directed psychiatric interviews she had been forced to attend, when she'd made it back to headquarters. Her boss, Chief Inspector Mark Johnson, the head of homicide in the state, was under intense pressure after word had got out to the media that the police's star homicide detective and her partner, Detective Sergeant Nick Vada, had been attacked and was now in a coma. And although the outcome would have been worse without her intervention, he reluctantly advised her that she needed to do five sessions with a counsellor to help talk through any issues she may have been having after the incident.

The nondescript office building was only a block away from the police headquarters and looked no different to the hundreds of others in the area. She walked up the black, tiled staircase and looked at the neat signage next to the bank of elevators for her destination. Level 6 held the offices of Doctor Lisa Bettleston – Licensed Clinical Mental Health Counsellor. Joanna tried not to groan. She'd done a few sessions like this in her earlier days on the force and had a general idea of how it would go down: who, when, and why. And the biggest question that was always asked – and how did that make you feel?

To be honest with herself, she wasn't exactly sure what the problem was. Some days she was angry, angry at her partner for going off gung-ho without asking for her help once again, disappointed that he had put himself in another dangerous situation, and she was scared. Most of all she was scared for Nick. He was still in a medically-induced coma in Morristown, nine hours south of Sydney, and apparently still too unstable to transport to a bigger, closer hospital. She had stuck around the hospital for another week once the case was wrapped up, unsure of what to do or where to go. She spent time with his sister Jess by his bedside, and spent time alone with him, confiding her deepest, darkest thoughts and worries, her self-doubt, and her anger at herself for not being able to protect him.

The counsellor had said the same things that Joanna had guessed she would have said. She asked about the days leading up to the night. The night itself; and the actual attack on Nick. She asked how she felt about it, how she felt about herself, and how his actions had affected their relationship.

It was something she hadn't thought about until that moment. How did his actions affect their relationship? She had been serious with him before the altercation. She had told him how his actions and pig headedness around running into dangerous situations had affected her and he had seemingly disregarded it. The more the counsellor spoke, the more she realised Nick's selfishness, and his lack of care for her feelings. This made her worry turn into anger, and that anger she directed back at the counsellor and her belief that they should have had more resources for their small rural division, and that the lack of resources was a contributing factor to his grave injuries.

They say therapy is completely private and confidential, but Joanna learned in the days after that first session, that that must not have been the case when she was pulled into the Chief Inspector's office on his day off, for a private word.

The Chief looked tired; more tired than usual, and she knew that his repeated trips south to visit Nick in hospital were starting to take a toll. He welcomed her in and she watched as he sat back down at his desk. His eyes were bloodshed and his face, usually clean-shaven, was a few days past that. He tapped his pen nervously on his desk and cleared his throat. 'Eh-erm.'

'You wanted to see me?' Joanna asked.

'I did,' the Chief replied. 'I did.' He looked past her, into the depths of the office and the people going about their work. Joanna could tell something was up. But she knew not to push. It was something she had learned from Nick. Sometimes silence is your friend. 'How have you been since you got back? I feel like I haven't seen much of you?'

The Chief was right. Joanna was avoiding head office like the plague. The pats on the back in congratulations for solving the murder of another cop were always good, but the 'so, so sorrys' about Nick were what she didn't want to hear. She didn't want to be treated like another victim. So, she chose to stay away. She had paperwork she could complete from home, away from prying eyes, so she chose to do that and await next instructions. 'Yeah, I've been alright. Laying low I guess.'

The Chief nodded. 'That's fair. I know you and Nick are the talk of the office right now.'

Hearing Nick's name made her flinch. 'All good talk, I hope.'

'You solved a cold case that no-one thought was going to be cracked.' The Chief pointed into the busy office. 'I'd given half this team a crack at it and none of them got close. You both did incredible work and you should be commended.'

Joanna smiled. 'But...? Why do I feel like there's a but coming?'

The Chief placed his pen down on the desk. 'I've got a copy of your psych evaluation that you completed the other day.'

'The confidential one?' she said, with a slight tone of sarcasm.

'Yes. Confidential.' The Chief cleared his throat again. 'Some damning stuff in here, Detective. You mind telling me some more about it?'

Joanna shrugged. 'I was angry. It was just me venting. I know you're in a tight spot, budgets and all that, I hear it from Nick all the time. I just felt like we were on our own out there. I feel like we are always on our own.'

The Chief frowned. 'Jo, you had over twenty members of the Australian Federal Police who seemingly owed you a favour. I think you and I both know you had more than enough help. I don't think it's me who you are angry with.'

Joanna felt her face getting hot and her eyes glistened with tears. She wanted to be strong. She didn't need the Chief to see how bad she was still hurting. 'I know,' was all she had to say in reply.

'Nick went off again, on his own, and put himself in serious danger. If he was awake right now, I'd be sitting at the foot of his hospital bed, not the first time may I remind you, and I'd be giving him a serious dressing down. What he did was stupid and was not your fault, Jo.' He looked her right in the eyes. 'None of this was your fault.'

Joanna wiped away a single tear, and then cleared her throat. 'So, what now?'

'Well. Now. Now we have everyone on our back watching us like hawks. The higher-ups are already looking into what happened at Blarnie and I think it won't be long before they get a copy of this transcript. So, we need to be prepared to talk to them if they ask.'

'I'm sorry,' Joanna replied.

'No need to be sorry. I agree with the things you said. Sometimes you just need to remember your audience.'

'Understood.' Silence fell between the pair and Joanna was the first to break it. 'So, what case do you want me on now?'

The Chief laughed out loud. 'A case? No case. I want you to take two weeks leave. No exceptions.'

Chapter Three

It was on the third day of her mandated leave that Joanna decided to do something. She tossed up whether to return to Morristown and be with Nick, but his sister Jess had facetimed and said that there was no news to report. Joanna wondered how much longer Jess would stick around. She had a newborn at home on her farm and a toddler to contend with. Maybe being with her brother was giving her a break, Joanna wondered.

She mulled over her options. She could sit and mope, spending her time worrying and wondering about all the dumb decisions she had made. She could drink. She had already drunk a bottle of red the afternoon before and the dull throbbing pain at the back of her head was a suggestion that she should try something else. She thought of her small friendship group. One of her best friends, Lilly Sanders, had become a brand-new mother only a few months earlier, and Joanna smiled and wondered how her friend would be handling motherhood. She couldn't exactly rock up on Lilly's doorstep in Melbourne with a bottle of wine like in the old days though.

Some of her other school friends had drifted away slowly, the way people do over the years. People grew up, with busy jobs and new families of their own. Her newer friends were all cops, cops she had met in her various stints around the state, and similar to her school friends, after each passing town, they too became a distant memory. She hadn't realised at the time, but partnering up with Nick and jumping into the deep end with her new role as a homicide detective was a lonely profession. Nick was now one of her closest friends.

She padded around her apartment in bare feet and her pyjamas. She opened her fridge and looked at another full bottle of wine and contemplated what the rest of her day would look like. She closed the door. She prided herself on her self-control. She was fitter than most, and had always been a relatively fussy eater, ensuring her body was in optimal condition for the work that she did. Bad food and too much alcohol were never going to be vices for her.

Her couch was still new and had that stiff unfamiliarity that all new furniture had. She sat down and pulled her phone out again to scroll social media. She rolled through the apps, looking at the best few seconds of each of her friends' days through the screen, wondering just what she was searching for when saw the next photo. Her little brother Benjamin, or Benji as she had called him since they were little kids, had posted a simple photo: an image of a sunset over what looked to be a cattle yard. She thought of her little brother, and tried to think of when the last time was that they had spoken. It had been a month earlier when she had wished him happy birthday and they'd shot a few fast texts through. They were a weird set of siblings. Their mother had died when they were young and they were both brought up by their alcoholic father. They had been inseparable, with Joanna taking on the role of being young Benji's carer while her father ran through odd jobs until his drinking put them into near homelessness.

She tapped on his profile and looked at the most recent photo of her little brother. He stood leaning against similar farm fencing to his sunset image. He was tall, he had their father's height where Joanna was short. He had dark brown almost black hair and was clean-shaven. His skin was tanned from the last few years spent out in the bush, and he looked happy. Content even.

She wondered what had caused them to drift apart. She knew deep down the answer was pretty simple. As soon as she was old enough to rent her own place she had moved out, working odd jobs to sustain herself while she studied at university, skipping between subjects, unsure on what her future career intentions were going to be. She couldn't afford to have Benji live with her for the first few years, and she knew her dad had taken a lot of anger out on him. By the time she felt financially able to support him he had already moved out and left home. It was funny, she thought to herself. Two kids who had grown up in the suburbs of Melbourne had both headed outwards, away from the hustle and bustle and deep into the bush. Benji had worked odd jobs: farmhand, tractor driver, truck driver, shearer, fencer. Every conversation she had with him over the years was always the same. Where are you? What are you doing? Are you okay? Do you need any money? Now, when she thought back, she realised she hadn't seen him face-to-face since he made a passing visit back in Milford before she became a detective.

Her thumb hovered over his name in her contact list. With this time off, she thought maybe he'd have some time to catch up with her. Wherever he was, it wasn't going to be in the city.

The phone rang three times and Benji answered. 'Afternoon. I was thinking about you the other day.'

'Oh, really?' It was good to hear his voice.

'Yeah. Read a news article about your partner. Up in the mountains. Were you involved in all of that?'

Benji had an inquisitive mind. She had always told him he would've made a great cop. 'Yeah, unfortunately I was.'

'He still in a bad way?'

'Yep. Still in a coma. Down in Morristown.' There was an uncomfortable silence between the pair and Joanna cleared her throat. 'Where are you right now?'

She could hear the sound of trucks in the background and men speaking. 'Me? Little town called Gabinda. Middle of bloody nowhere, out near Bourke. Surprised my phone's working out here, but locals reckon Optus just put a new tower in.'

Gabinda. She hadn't heard of it. 'What brings you out there?'

Benji laughed. 'You wouldn't believe it, Sis. You are talking to a trainee bull rider. I'm following the rodeos. Joined on with a big crew that's based just out of town.'

'Bull riding?' Joanna wasn't shocked. Benji would try anything, he had a daredevil streak to him and, annoyingly for her, seemed to pick things up quicker than most. 'Sounds dangerous.'

'Nah. It's not too bad. Plenty of gear these days, helmets, padded vests and all that. I'll be alright.'

Joanna had opened up a map on her iPad while they spoke. She looked up Gabinda and how far away she was from there.

Seven hours. 'Hey, I know this is a bit random, but I've got some time off. How about I come up your way and we catch up?'

'To Gabinda? Jo, I don't know, it's a long drive.'

'I've got nothing else going on, Benj. It'll be good to see you. It's been too long. Plus, I want to see my little brother get thrown off a bull. Might be a good laugh.'

Benji chuckled. 'Alright then. The rodeo goes over two days, the big event is tonight. I'm sleeping behind the stockyards in a mate's trailer, but I'll get you a room at the pub if you'd like?'

Joanna laughed to herself. Even on leave she was travelling out into the bush and staying in pub rooms. 'Thanks.' She looked at the clock on her wall. It was 9 am. 'Sounds good. Seven-hour drive from my place. I'll see you sometime this afternoon. I'll call you when I get close.'

***

The drive had been enjoyable. Joanna felt revitalised having made plans, something concrete that she could work towards. She had stuffed some clothes into her travel bag and closed up her place. She was used to being ready to leave at a moment's notice from work, so this was no different. She wanted to get there before the sun went down as she hated driving at night with all the kangaroos that could pop up on the road. That was always Nick's job; his reaction time and reading of the road ahead was always better than hers.

The city had slowly disappeared in her rear view and she realised as she got further and further away that an invisible weight was slowly beginning to lift off her shoulders. All of her worry for Nick and what was going to happen was still there, but she somehow felt calm and at peace being back out in nature, back out in the bush where she knew Nick would want her to be. She stopped for a quick bite for lunch at a small bakery on the outskirts of Dubbo and then made the last two hundred kilometres towards Gabinda in good time. The showgrounds were on the southern side of town and Benji had sent her a Google Maps pin that she headed towards. She turned off the main highway that looked to continue on through the township and slowed along a narrow dirt road. The road seemed to be a boundary between thick bushland and the vast wheat farmland that continued on into the distant horizon.

The showgrounds materialised in the distance after a few more minutes and she realised she was arriving into the back area of where the rodeo arena was. Semi-trucks and trailers along with motorhomes and caravans were spread out along the roadside everywhere, and she slowed down to walking pace when she spotted kids out near the road playing on bikes.

She texted Benji that she had arrived and he directed her to park behind the big red road train, the last truck of the row. She was in Nick's unmarked BMW police car and, going by the suspicious looks of the people at the campground, it may as well have had sirens on the top of it. She got out and stretched her arms above her head, feeling the last of the day's heat beating down on her neck. She was tight and a little tired from the drive but when Benji popped around the corner, ran over and gave her a big hug, she knew she'd made the right decision to get out of town.

He was thinner than she remembered as she felt the hardened muscles across his back and shoulders. When he pulled back to look at her with a wide smile, she could see that he was beginning to age. There were creases and fine wrinkles around his eyes that she had never seen before.

'Sis! I see you haven't grown,' he said jovially as he patted her head. Her height was always a source of amusement for him.

She smiled. 'Still trying.' She wrapped her hand around one of his biceps. 'You eating? You're skin and bone.'

Benji held both arms up and flexed. 'It's all muscle, sis.' He turned around and pointed towards the light towers and high metal stands around the arena. 'Welcome to the show.'

Chapter Four

It was the smell of lime that was the first thing that floated into his mind. Lime hospital disinfectant. The room was warm, warmer than what he was used to, and he could feel heat radiating from his body through the thin blanket that was draped over him. Everything was black, and remained black as his mind searched through bits and pieces of memories old and new. Could he smell the sea as well? Was he near Riema, the coastal town where his holiday home was? Or was he still in the Cobar hospital near Secret? His mind would blank whenever he'd try to pin down any detail, and the thoughts would slowly dissolve again.

The beginnings of consciousness seemed to float in and out, like the rolling waves of the ocean, and there were now a few moments where he willed his brain to allow himself to wake – but nothing happened. He could hear a voice speaking to him from his bedside. It was a woman's, and it was warm and kind. It took him another day to realise that this woman was his sister,

Jess. How had she got to Cobar? His memory was only of burning his hand and hitting his head? From the beeps of monitors and the hiss of another machine he couldn't quite place, it seemed much more serious than what he could remember.

***

Joanna left her car parked beside the hulking road train and followed her brother towards the front of a state-of-the-art, shining new motorhome. It was a highly polished white with the image of a bucking bull on the side, and the giant chrome wheels glistened in the sunlight.

'I'll introduce you to Neville. This is his bus,' Benji said, pointing to the motorhome. 'He runs the riding team I'm currently on. He runs things around here.'

At that moment a hiss emanated from the tinted glass door as it opened and a tall man in his late fifties stepped out. He wore leather riding chaps that had red ornate patterns sewed into the sides of them, and he had a well-worn black Akubra cowboy hat on. He turned and saw Benji and a big smile spread across his face that went right up to his eyes. 'Benji!'

'Hey boss,' Benji replied. He pointed to Joanna. 'I wanted to introduce you to someone.'

'That right?' The cowboy stepped down off the bottom step of the bus and ambled towards them. His gait was awkward, and he had a prominent limp that caused his left leg to drag slightly in the dirt. He reached Joanna and took her hand. 'Neville Ford. Pleasure to meet you, miss.'

'This is Joanna,' Benji added. 'She's my sister.'

'Nice to meet you, Neville,' Joanna replied.

Neville patted Benji on the shoulder. 'Joanna, has Benji told you that he's my next big thing? Might get Rookie of the Year if he plays his cards right!'

Joanna could see genuine affection in Benji's eyes as he looked at the man. Like a father figure, a real father figure that he never really had. She could see why he was so passionate now about giving this a shot. 'Benji hasn't told me a lot of things,' she said. She looked over to the arena. 'When's the show start?'

Neville turned towards the bright lights that had turned on as night fell. He looked down at his watch. 'Roping and barrel racers go first. We're the big show. Couple of hours away.' A walkie-talkie attached to his belt chirped and he replied into it. 'Got to go. It was nice meeting you, Joanna, we'll catch up later. Benji, I'll see you over at pen three?'

Benji gave his boss the thumbs up as he walked away. 'Come on, come meet the guys.'

There was a group that was beginning to emerge from the trailers and caravans as they walked towards the arena. Men stretching their arms above their heads, fresh from afternoon naps. Another one swigging from a bottle of Jack Daniels as he rested on the tailgate of a red Holden ute. Joanna watched one kiss his wife on the lips and then bend down and tussle a little boys hair. A father off to work again, except this father's job was more dangerous than most.

The crowd near the cattle yards thinned and Joanna spotted a group of men spread out around the base of a tree. Benji walked in their direction and stopped when they all looked up at his arrival. 'Boys, this is my sister Joanna. She's come out of the big city for her first-ever rodeo experience.' Joanna went to correct him, she had spent just as much time in the bush as him, but thought better of it. Benji pointed to the men one by one. The first man, leaning against the tree, wore a black Akubra the same style as her brother's, black chaps and a light blue checked shirt. He had a cigarette dangling out of the side of his mouth and a serious expression. 'That's Dean, he's our old man of the group. He's been on the tour the longest. Eleventh year, Dean?'

'Twelfth,' Dean replied gruffly. He stepped forward and shook Joanna's hand. His hand was huge and his palms were as rough as sandpaper. 'Pleasure to meet you, Joanna.'

Benji pointed to the next man beside him, 'That's Glenn.'

Glenn held out his hand and Joanna shook it. He had sandy blond hair underneath his black Akubra. His eyes were green and piercing and he had a scar that ran from his left eye to the corner of his lopsided smile. He looked like an old-fashioned movie star. She tried not to blush as his eyes shone into hers. 'Nice to meet you,' she said.

The last man in the group didn't offer his hand but gave her a muted wave. He looked to be the youngest of the men and she could tell by his reluctance to speak. She could feel apprehension in his body language. He was tall and gangly and didn't even look like he'd started shaving yet. 'Bryce,' he said in a low voice.

'Bryce here is our youngest on the tour. He's been killing it over the last few months, working his way up the rankings.'

Joanna nodded in the young man's direction. 'Nice to meet you all.' She could feel her stomach grumbling after the long drive. 'Anywhere where I can find something to eat? I'm starved.'

Benji pointed in the direction of the Ferris wheel. 'Sure. As long as you like show food. Try the blue caravan at the end, George has the best stuff. Healthiest anyway.'

The group seemed to agree with Benji's assessment, so Joanna was convinced. 'Alright then, I'm going to grab something. You hungry?'

Benji looked at his watch. 'I struggle to eat before I ride. But yeah, I'll come for a walk.'

The arena was slowly beginning to fill up as the locals from the showgrounds made their way to the next spot of entertainment. Young kids sat in the bottom rows of the bleachers, all fascinated with the view from behind the high metal fencing. There was a big screen propped up high on scaffolding and as Joanna and Benji walked past she watched as a woman riding a brown horse at incredible speed roped a small poddy calf in one swift motion.

'Incredible,' Joanna commented on the show of athleticism.

Benji laughed. 'That's Kasey Cochrane. One of the best female horseback riders we got.'

They continued on past the arena into the area with all the show rides. The neon lights from the dodgem cars cast brilliant light across the red dirt between Joanna and her brother. She watched him closely as he walked. She was glad she made the trip. He seemed happy to see her and they seemed to have fallen straight back into step with each other without too many words spoken. She knew that there would always be an uncertain undertone with their relationship, but she didn't have the emotional battery to deal with any conversations like that at the moment. Nick had already drained her enough.

The line for the blue caravan that Benji had spoken of was long, which was a good sign to Joanna. The food on the menu sounded delicious. Chicken schnitzel salad wraps, Vietnamese-style roast pork rolls with crackling, even an acai bowl was mentioned. Joanna was surprised; show food was always deep fried: dagwood dogs, dim sims, a woodfire pizza truck if you were lucky. Her mouth watered at the thought of her early dinner.

She felt a jolt from behind and turned to see a young boy with his arms wrapped around Benji's waist.

'Oi!' Benji said with a chuckle. 'Where's your mum?'

The young boy spun around and pointed behind them both. A man and woman stood three people back from them. The woman looked to be about Joanna's age and was wearing denim jeans and a denim jacket. She had dark hair, almost black, and it ran down over her shoulders. She gave them a shy wave. 'Benji,' she said.

Benji spoke to the person behind them pointing to the woman. 'Save our spot for two seconds?'

The person in line nodded and Benji ushered Joanna to follow as he introduced them. 'Joanna, this is Gabby, Gabby this is my sister Joanna.'

Joanna's radar went up as her eyes travelled over the man beside Gabby. He was tall, a foot taller than the three of them and she could see a tribal tattoo running up his neck. He spat on the ground to the left of the group and looked in Benji's direction. 'Benji,' he said.

'Cameron,' Benji replied.

The young boy stood over to the side and spoke up. 'Benji, are you going to ride Bandsaw tonight?'

Joanna looked at the young boy. He looked like he was ten or eleven years old. He was tall and thin and had a red t-shirt and a black cap with the Chicago Bulls basketball team logo on it. He looked right on the precipice of being a teenager, not still a boy and not a man yet. 'This is Matty,' Benji said to Joanna. 'You're gonna be a bull rider one day too, aren't you?'

The young boy yelled, 'Yep!'

Cameron scoffed and turned away from the group, walking off towards the arena, speaking on his phone. Gabby seemed uncomfortable. She shrugged. 'Old memories, I guess.'

'Cameron used to ride,' Benji filled Joanna in. 'A long time ago.'

***

Joanna sat and ate her chicken schnitzel wrap as Benji got dressed for the big show. He clipped his leather chaps over his Wrangler jeans and got out his helmet and padded vest. Joanna took a sip of water and pointed back towards the showgrounds. 'That woman, Gabby. How do you know her?'

Benji smiled. 'She's a nurse. She's treated a few of us.'

'That all she is?' Joanna asked.

Benji looked at her. 'What's that supposed to mean?'

Joanna laughed. 'C'mon. I saw the way you looked at her. Have you two ever been an item?'

Benji shook his head. 'Nah, no chance of that.'

Chapter Five

After her quick dinner, Benji had advised Joanna he needed to head to the riders briefing, so she took herself for a walk through the showgrounds before making her way to the arena for the night session of bull riding.

As she sat in the stands she looked across at the crowd, there were all sorts mixed throughout. She could tell the farming families, she could pick them out the quickest, she could also tell who the town folk were. She was learning to be more observant in day-to-day life, she knew that it could help with her police work, to watch and study the way people interacted with each other.

The family Benji introduced her to in the food line sat only a few rows below her and she watched the back of them as the couple spoke. Benji didn't offer much more information after their chance meeting, but she had watched her brother as he looked back at the woman a few times in the line. Even though he denied it, she still wondered if there was something there.

The bull riding rounds began and the attitude of the crowd became more boisterous. The announcer's energy was high, reaching fever pitch, and she began to feel her own level of excitement mixed with trepidation rise at the thought of her brother riding the huge beasts that came thundering out of the stalls. She watched as a man in red came flying out of the stalls as the bull spun and kicked ferociously. His grip was true and he moved with grace as the announcer's loud play by play description came through the speakers. 'Glenn Copeland! One of the best we got! Look at him go!'

Joanna realised the rider was one of the men Benji had introduced her to, the one who looked like a movie star. It seemed his skills backed up his looks as he let go of the rope from the bull with incredible athleticism. He was launched upwards, and as the bull continued on forward towards the clowns, he landed dead flat on his feet as the crowd roared. He gave a gracious bow and nodded in Joanna's direction with a tip of hat. She looked behind herself and at the people beside her. *Was he looking at me?* she wondered.

'Alright, everyone, next up we have a crowd favourite and current Rookie of the Year contender, Bryce Young! Bryce shot the lights out in the qualifiers earlier today.'

Joanna looked down at the gate where the next bull was due to go out, she could see Dean, the elder statesman of the group hitting young Bryce on the shoulders of his padded vests, giving him a rev up. Across from him was Benji who looked to be speaking words of encouragement.

The announcer continued. 'Bryce Young is up next and has drawn a short straw in my opinion, he'll be riding one of the meanest buggers of the night, Bandsaw, a relative of one of Australia's most famous bulls, Chainsaw.'

Joanna didn't know what made a bull good or bad, but going by the footage that was playing over the screens, the bull called Bandsaw could throw riders off left and right and any which way it wanted. She watched on in anticipation as the gate flew open and Bryce and Bandsaw shot out under the bright lights. All seemed well at first as Bryce rhythmically followed the kicks and spins of Bandsaw with a deft touch. As the eight second digital timer on the screen neared its end she watched on in horror as the bull kicked up at an awkward angle at the perfect moment.

As the tip of the horn jammed up under Bryce's helmet and crashed through his jaw she stood up out of her seat in horror. His limp body had hardly hit the ground as she looked across the arena towards the carpark for an ambulance. There were screams from the crowd as she looked down and she watched as Glenn and then Dean jumped the high fence and sprinted into the arena as the two rodeo clowns ushered Bandsaw back through one of the gates.

She ran down to the tier of seating that Gabby and Cameron sat in. 'You're a nurse, aren't you?'

'Yeah,' Gabby replied.

'Come on! Let's go see if we can help him!'

Joanna jogged down the steep aluminium steps and looked back as Gabby stood up and followed. She reached the fence line at the same time as Benji who opened a section and the two women ran through. She let Gabby take the lead. She was trained in emergency situations like this, but she knew if Gabby was a nurse she could handle a violent injury like this better than most.

Joanna took one look at Bryce's face and took a step back. She couldn't look at it. It made her feel sick. Her mind, so used to seeing gore, had seemed to be unprepared during civilian life. She turned and looked at Benji.

Benji seemed to notice his sister's aversion. 'Hey Jo, come on, come and direct the ambulance in with me, could ya?'

Joanna was happy to get away. She jogged over to the edge of the barriers with her brother as she heard sirens entering the showgrounds. As she walked through the gate she heard a loud grunt and bang of the metal fencing to her left. She looked on through the fencing at Bandsaw who was staring her down and seemed to be sizing her up. She couldn't believe the sheer size of the animal, he was double her height easily and she couldn't comprehend how any person would want to get up on top of him and ride him.

'Hey! Hey! Over here!' Benji yelled out as an older style Ford F250 ambulance slowed to navigate the tricky turn between the fencing.

They waved the ambulance workers through and followed it back, allowing them to take over from Gabby who seemed to be doing a good job. Joanna watched as Bryce was transferred to a stretcher and then lifted up and placed into the ambulance. His left hand lifted and his thumb slowly came up, to the cheers and clapping of the crowd. She couldn't believe the young man's bravery. As far as she was concerned, he had nearly been killed.

Looking on from the ambulance, Joanna could see Cameron had arrived on the scene and seemed to be gesturing wildly towards the showgrounds. They seemed to be arguing about something. Joanna looked over to Benji who shrugged. Gabby spun around, spotted the two of them and then ran over in their direction. 'Benji. Cameron can't find Matty. Can you give us a hand to have a look around?'

Benji looked back towards the crowd that was slowly leaving, and then towards the cattle yards. It seemed that for now the rodeo was over. 'Yeah, of course,' he said. 'Jo's a cop, she'll be able to help.'

Joanna gave her brother a look. She didn't need to be off running around looking for kids. Especially a kid who in her opinion looked old enough to be looking after himself. She was tired from the long drive and all the night's action. But Gabby looked concerned, so she nodded in agreeance. 'Where did you see him last?'

Cameron spoke for the couple. 'He was sitting in the stands with us. He told me he wanted to go get an ice cream, I told him it shouldn't be a problem.'

'Has he got any friends here?' Joanna asked.

'Yeah. Some school friends, I think.'

Joanna looked towards the show alley. 'C'mon, let's head towards the rides. He could be there with his friends.'

Gabby turned and set off towards the alley as the group followed. Joanna caught up to Cameron and looked upwards to speak to the man. 'Has he got a phone?'

'Tried it,' Cameron replied. 'It's ringing out.'

A good start with it still being on, Joanna thought to herself. Phones can be tracked. If worse came to worse and the police needed to get involved, they could always request that data. She prayed it didn't need to get to that.

The rides section was a wide strip of land filled left and right with various rides. She looked to the left: the Zipper, the Chacha, the Hurricane, dodgem cars and a shooting gallery all ran along the left side. She looked across to the right. The music trip, a fun house, a giant inflatable worm, a jumping castle and a dilapidated looking haunted house spanned that side.

'I'll try the haunted house and the fun house,' Benji said to the group and set off.

Joanna walked towards the Hurricane ride and watched the carriages as the next ride slowed. She turned back to Gabby. She remembered he was wearing a red shirt, but wondered if he had any other distinguishing features. 'What was he wearing again? Describe his whole outfit.'

Gabby closed her eyes momentarily. 'Ahhh. Red shirt, denim shorts, he had blue and red sneakers on that the heels would light up if you pressed them a certain way.'

'He had a black cap as well,' Cameron added. 'It had the Chicago Bulls logo on it.'

Joanna logged it all into her memory bank. 'Alright, I'm going to head down the end of the row towards the ice cream stand, ask if they served him. You two see if you can find his friends and ask them if they've seen him.'

Chapter Six

It may have been a few days, or merely a few hours later, but the memory of why he lay in the hospital bed finally returned to him. He remembered the darkened path and he remembered seeing the woman in trouble. The knife blade sticking out of her stomach. He remembered the fear in her eyes. Was it the fear of death? Or fear that the person who hurt her would do the same to him? He wasn't sure.

The cold was his final memory. The chill of the damp earth that he lay on and the bright lights and speckled dots that filled his vision as he tried to maintain consciousness. He willed his mind to remember anything else, and he finally remembered the voice of his partner, Joanna. She came to him like a thunderbolt. 'Nick, Nick you will be okay. I've got you,' were the words he remembered. It was a comforting feeling knowing that she had been there for him.

A voice floated through the darkness. 'We've upped his medication, we are trying a new drug that's been used in the States. They've had great results. Also, we need to keep up the stimulation plan and physical therapy that's been happening. Hearing, touch, smell, taste and vision. They all need to be individually worked on. Someone is still there, we can see that on the brain scans. I unfortunately just can't tell you who that person will be until he wakes up.'

***

The crowd had now mostly left the stands of the rodeo arena and seemed to all be in the fairgrounds now. The ride lines were jam-packed with people and Joanna scanned each line as best as she could as she headed towards the food area. Benji came running up and put his hand on her shoulder. 'Nothing in the haunted house or fun house. I just called Neville and he has put a call in to the show organiser, Garry Toohey. He's headed this way with as many people as he can muster, they can help look. We'll get an announcement over the loudspeaker as well.'

'Great idea. Good thinking.'

They both stopped out front of the ice cream van. It was a vintage, 50s-style Airstream trailer painted in a garish bright pink. The line was short and Joanna waited as the last child walked away happily with a towering choc mint ice cream in a cone. The man who was serving looked to be in his early sixties and had a bald head that shone under the light above. His apron was bright white and he held his scoop at the ready. 'Help you?'

'Not looking for ice cream, sorry. We have a lost boy. He was supposedly headed here. Eleven years old. Red shirt, black cap and denim shorts. By any chance have you served anyone like that?'

The man looked over Joanna towards the crowd, seemingly lost in thought. 'It's been a busy night, sorry. I may have, I just can't remember right now.'

'You got a pen?'

The man flipped a napkin in her direction and handed her a pen. She wrote her number down quickly, she could see the line behind them was starting to get restless, and then slid it back to him. 'His name is Matty. If you spot anyone matching that description, please call me straightaway?'

'Will do.'

They turned away from the van together and walked back in the direction of the show rides. Joanna looked across at Benji. 'How many people do you think are here?'

Benji shrugged. 'Nev reckons they sold 1,500 tickets just for the rodeo itself. I'd say over 2,000 at least, rodeo isn't everybody's cup of tea.'

Joanna looked across the expanse of people, she hadn't dealt with many missing kids before but knew during training that the first twenty-four hours were always critical. Major mistakes made during those first few hours could mean life or death. She didn't want to sound too dire around anyone, but she was beginning to get the feeling they had a serious problem.

'C'mon, let's go find Gabby,' she said.

Gabby and Cameron were in the same spot that she'd left them, but this time a group of young boys and girls had joined the fray, along with some older people who looked to be fellow parents. Joanna reached them first and Gabby's eyebrows rose expectantly, like she was about to receive some amazing news. 'Any luck?' Gabby asked.

Joanna shook her head. 'He hadn't seen him.'

Tears streamed down Gabby's face. 'I don't understand. Where could he have gone? It was only a few minutes.'

Joanna looked at the rest of the group. 'Has anyone seen Matty in the last few hours?'

One young boy held up his hand. 'I saw him standing over there.' He pointed to the small dirt path that led towards the entrance. He then pointed to Benji. 'He was talking to a cowboy like him.'

Benji looked down at the clothes he was wearing. 'What colour were his clothes?' he asked.

The boy shrugged. 'I only remembered his hat. He wore a black one.'

Joanna made a mental note. It wasn't much, but it was a start. 'Thank you. I say we spread out again and keep looking. He could still be around here somewhere.'

The group fanned out again, seemingly buoyed by the small snippet of information. Joanna got out her phone and called the state switchboard. It might be too soon, but she decided that it was better to be safe than sorry.

'Dispatch, here.'

'Evening, this is Detective Joanna Gray with Rural Homicide. I'm out at Gabinda and we have a missing child. Can you please connect me to the local station?'

A series of clicks and beeps came through the speaker and then a woman's voice came down the line. 'Gabinda station, this is Sergeant Amelia Rossi.'

'Amelia, this is Detective Joanna Gray with Rural Homicide. I'm in town right now at your local show and I think we have a spot of bother here. Missing boy, Matty....' She looked over at Benji, hoping for a prompt of a last name. Blackwood, Benji mouthed. 'Blackwood. Matty Blackwood,' she finished.

She could hear typing coming through the speaker and an urgent shout out. 'Blackwood, you say? Let me call the local Inspector, he's not in at the moment. I'll head down right away. There's another local truck out and about, I'll get him there straightaway to assist. Is it okay if I send your number to the Inspector?'

'Of course. Thank you,' Joanna replied and then hung up.

Benji grinned. 'It's about to be an absolute circus here now.'

Joanna was confused. 'What do you mean by that?'

'The Blackwood's own this town. John Blackwood owns 'Moroco'. It's one of the biggest farms in the state out this way.'

'How do you know that?'

'Gabinda's our home base,' Benji replied. 'Neville has a farm here, it's a training facility for bull riders. One of the biggest in the state. He's got a big bunkhouse, everyone's welcome. I stay here from time to time. Been coming here for years. Been coming here since …' he stopped himself.

'Since you left Dad?'

Benji nodded. 'One of the first places I called home. Neville took me in. Looked after me like another son.'

It was all slowly coming together for Joanna, her little brother's life on from when she left. It was romantic in a way. A young boy, lost and without a home, brought in by a generous property owner he saw as a fatherly figure. She snapped her thoughts back to the present. 'So, Gabby's the Blackwood? Or Cameron?'

'Gabby.'

'So Matty Blackwood is John Blackwood's grandson?'

'Yep. John's a good man, I've worked out at Moroco a few times. He's a tough old bugger, he calls it how it is. And when he finds out his grandson is missing, shit will hit the fan.'

Chapter Seven

Nestled among the sprawling flat paddocks, the old homestead was a forgotten time capsule of yesteryear. It was a single storey home, made of stone and mud rock back in the 1800s, capped off with a corrugated iron roof that had been recently replaced with sparkling bright white Colorbond iron. A verandah wrapped right around the property that was shaded by a single giant palm tree, which was planted by its owners in the 1950s.

John Blackwood, the owner of the homestead sat in a high-backed wicker chair with a beer in hand. Harvest preparation was in full swing but with incoming rain it was looking like they would be stuck waiting until it passed. He had found it hard to switch off this year and relax with how much work there was still to be done. The sound of the rugby game that was on in the lounge room floated into his ears and he tried to hear the score. His team had had a terrible year, and going by the commentary, it didn't sound like this game was going any better.

The house was always a hive of activity, and he struggled to remember a time he had ever been home alone. His son, Casey Blackwood, was off at the local show with his wife and their granddaughter. He sipped his beer again and looked out at the starlit sky. The show was always a good bit of fun but he hadn't felt up to it that night for some reason. The rodeo had been on and he'd always enjoyed watching Neville's squad of misfits running themselves into the ground. His phone rang on the table beside him and he placed his beer down, frustrated at whoever was upsetting his peace.

He looked at the name on the screen. It was his daughter Gabby. Why would she be calling him, he wondered. He hadn't spoken to her in years, why would tonight be any different? He let it go to voicemail and picked up his cold bottle of beer again.

The phone rang again and he cursed under his breath. Whatever it was, it must have been important. 'Gabby,' he answered in a neutral tone.

His daughter sounded frantic. 'Dad. We're at the showgrounds. Matty is missing. I know I shouldn't be calling you. I don't know what to do.'

John stood up. 'Whereabouts at the showgrounds? Who are you with? How long has he been missing?'

'We were at the rodeo. At the arena in the stands. We were watching the show. He just went to get an ice cream. Cameron—'

'That fuckwit let him go off on his own?' John fumed. His daughter's dropkick partner was one of the main reasons they hadn't spoken in a few years. Once a criminal, always a criminal, he always said.

'Dad, I was there too. It wasn't his fault. I'm just asking for help; I don't want to fight.'

John headed into the kitchen and grabbed the keys to one of his utes. 'I'll be there in thirty minutes. Casey is there too I'm pretty sure. I'll call him. Have you called Archie?'

'No. There's a policewoman here though, Remember Benji Gray? It's his sister. She's a detective, apparently. She's helping.'

That sounded promising, John thought. He'd known Archie, the local police inspector in town, since they were kids. He was as useless as tits on a bull. He had a couple of younger officers who seemed to have more brains, but he knew that having a detective from out of town – someone who had actually dealt with stuff like this before – would be a big help. 'Alright, I'm on my way.'

His Toyota Landcruiser roared down the long dirt driveway of his farm. Moroco had been in the Blackwood family for six generations. His family had come off a boat in the late 1800s from Ireland and had somehow ended up in Gabinda of all places and had laid down roots. His great-grandfather and grandfather had been the driving forces behind Moroco's growth. As other farmers had dropped away during the world wars, they had motored on forward, buying more and more land until Moroco was one of the biggest properties in the state. Even the more recent extreme weather changes hadn't affected them as badly as other areas in the region. John remembered his grandfather telling him their family motto as a kid: 'You're a Blackwood, luck always falls our way.'

That's why, as he pushed his wagon well over the speed limit down the main highway towards the showgrounds, he wasn't overly concerned. Although he hadn't spoken to Gabby in a few years, young Matty had been allowed to come out onto the farm and spend time with him. The young boy was quiet, a little soft for his liking being a town kid, but he was the only male Blackwood grandchild he had. His son Casey had a two-year old daughter and seemed to have no plans on having any more. If John had his way, one day young Matty would be the heir to their property which was worth millions.

He pressed the top number in his favourites list and listened to the ringing through his Bluetooth speakers. 'Dad,' his son Casey answered.

'Case. Gabby just called me. You still at the show?'

'I am. I heard the news. One of Neville's bull riders told me. Me and Tori are just heading towards the rides now, I think they've got a little search party together.'

'Alright. Can you call the pub? If Paul and Norrie are there, I want them at the ground looking for him too, before I get there.'

'On it,' Casey replied.

Paul and Norrie were two of John's best workers on the farm. Paul was third in charge behind Casey and John, and John had known him since he was a young bloke. Norrie was their lone truckie, he did any grain or fertiliser carting that the farm needed when John didn't want to subcontract out.

John tapped his fingers on the steering wheel impatiently as the traffic slowed as cars left the showgrounds. He looked at the digital clock on his dashboard that read 9:00 pm. It was getting late and any of these cars leaving could have his grandson in them. He dialled the number for Archie, the local inspector, and waited.

'John?' came Archie's voice down the end of the phone line.

'Evening Archie. I'm sure you've heard the news by now?'

'I have. I've got a local truck there now, and my Sergeant is on her way. There's a Sydney D there who is giving us a hand also. I'm sure we'll find him quickly.'

'Archie, there's thirty fuckin' cars leaving this place every five minutes! He could be in one of 'em right now! Can't you set up a roadblock or something?' John thought he heard a scoff through the phone. 'What was that?' he asked.

'Nothing,' Archie replied. 'John, it's been three hours. Let's not turn this into something bigger than it is. He's probably propped up at a friend's house playing video games.'

'This is my fuckin' grandson you're speaking about, Inspector. If I tell you I think it's serious, I think it's bloody serious. Need I remind you all of the things I've done for you and this community?'

There was silence at the other end of the line. The Blackwood family owned nearly half of Gabinda. John's charitable donations had rebuilt the local primary school when it had burnt down, and was also one of the main reasons the Gabinda Show and Rodeo continued to happen, as John's donations had kept the gates open.

'Look, I'm near Dubbo at the moment, I have a family thing with my wife. If you don't find him tonight, which I'm sure you will, I'll be there first thing tomorrow morning to help lead the charge.'

John was satisfied. He just wanted the Inspector to know his place. 'Alright.' He pressed the end button on the call.

The showgrounds were still busy and he could see the bright lights of the Ferris wheel in the distance circulating lazily. Another ride was shooting people high in the air in their carriages and he could hear joyous screams. John pulled up as close as he could to the mouth of the show alley and made his way into the crowd. He could see where a group had formed near the food trucks and he walked up to it.

A short woman in dark denim jeans and a white t-shirt stood on a haybale. She was young, he guessed around early to mid-thirties and was pretty in a conventional way. She was tanned and he could see the muscle definition on her arms: she didn't look like someone to be messed with. Her dark hair was tied up in a high ponytail and she was speaking with authority. He assumed she was the detective that Gabby had spoken about.

She held up an image on an iPad that was blown up as much as possible. 'Alright everyone, this is Matty Blackwood. Last seen about three hours ago over there.' She pointed to an opening in the metal stands at the rodeo arena. 'He left those stands supposedly to get ice cream from the vendor right behind us. We have spoken with the vendor and he has said Matty never made it. Let's all spread out as much as possible, we want to try and cover as much ground as we can. We are hoping he hasn't gone far.'

Chapter Eight

Joanna lay down on the bunk bed mattress in the front section of the caravan, mentally and physically drained from the last few hours.

She, along with help from the show organiser, a softly spoken man named Garry Toohey, had managed to accumulate a decent amount of people for their search. They had spread out quickly, looking everywhere and anywhere they could. More and more people arrived, seemingly prepared to search all night if they had to, until the young boy was found.

Two local police officers from the Gabinda Police Station had introduced themselves, a Constable Thomas Webb and a Sergeant Amelia Rossi and had explained they'd arrived as soon as they could. Thomas had been at a domestic disturbance on the other side of town. That explained why the ambulance had left the arena, Joanna had noted in her mind. Once pleasantries were exchanged there wasn't much more to say other than 'good luck' as they joined the search parties.

They had searched high and low and as the clock struck midnight Joanna could feel the exasperation and dejection of the group set in. Some people began to head to their cars, unsure on how much more help they could be. Joanna knew that it had been five hours, and the young boy could be close by or nearly in Queensland by now. She knew she could work better with a clearer mind tomorrow after some sleep and went to find Benji. He was standing underneath the arena's metal bleachers talking to a tall man in a black Akubra.

The man was speaking animatedly to Benji and he stopped suddenly as Joanna got close. She cleared her throat awkwardly. 'Sorry was I interrupting?'

'Not at all,' the man replied. He stepped forward out of the darkness and the blinding lights of the arena shone down on him. He looked to be in his sixties and was tall and lean. He stretched out a hand to shake Joanna's and as she took it, she eyed the scars and sunspots on the arm of a man who had clearly spent his life on the land.

'Joanna Gray,' she said, introducing herself.

'You're the detective?' the man asked.

She nodded. 'Rural homicide.'

'John Blackwood,' he replied. 'I'm Matty's grandfather.'

Joanna took a closer look at the man. Although she could tell he was a hardened man of the land, she could still see the polish of someone quite wealthy: highly shined RM Williams boots, crisp moleskin pants and a silver diver's watch that looked like it belonged more in the city than in the bush. 'Nice to meet you, John. I'm sorry it's under these circumstances. I've spoken with Sergeant Rossi and she assures me that the Gabinda Police will do everything in their power to find young Matty.'

John scoffed at her reply. 'You're based out of Sydney aren't you Detective? I'm sure you're well aware of the standard of coppers that get sent all the way out into the sticks for us country mob.'

Although she felt offended at the comment, she was tired, and she knew the man was clearly distressed with his grandson missing, so she wasn't going to bite. She chose to ignore the comment. 'I'm going to call it for the night. Benji. Any chance I can bunk in with you? I'm absolutely wrecked.'

John Blackwood stepped closer and held his hand out. In between his two fingers was a money clip, an inch thick with green one-hundred-dollar notes. 'Help us here, Detective. Please.

Take this. For the investigation. If you need any more, you come straight back to me? I want to know where my grandson is.'

Joanna looked at the money in his hand and gently pushed it back towards him. She wasn't for sale. It went against everything she had ever worked for. Just the notion of trying to buy her put her on edge. 'I'm not for sale, Mr Blackwood.'

The exchange was terse and as Joanna lay in her bunk bed looking up at the slats of the bunk above, she wondered if she had her way again whether she would have said anything different. Her head swam with an overload of information and she closed her eyes, willing herself to get some sleep before the first rays of sunshine began to creep through the narrow caravan windows.

***

The next morning she woke up early to the sound of her brother snoring loudly. She stood up and stretched and then grabbed all her belongings from the caravan and stepped out into the morning sunrise.

The car park behind the arena remained full and she looked out across the vast expanse of caravans, cars, utes, trucks and trailers. The young boy could be in one of them right now. He could be anywhere, she mused. She opened her phone up and noted no missed calls or messages, which indicated that he had not been found. Besides, Benji would know by now if he was, and would've said something.

She looked over towards the trailer propped up at the end of the row. It was one of those music festival trailers that had toilets and showers in it, usually overflowing with terrible smells and lacking in toilet paper and soap. It would have to do. The red dust had caked on her face, and she could feel that the thick layer of foundation which normally covered her burn scars was almost gone. She felt naked without it. She walked over to Nick's car, *'Well, my car now'*, she thought, opened it up and grabbed her small sports bag out from the back seat.

The showers were empty and, once she confirmed there was hot water, spent time having a well-deserved, long, hot shower. She dried herself, put on a change of clothes and headed back towards her car feeling reinvigorated. It was only sunrise but the heat of the day was already starting to rise, and as she switched on the car she turned the fan on the AC on to its maximum setting. She flicked the stalk on the wiper to move the half inch of thick red dust that was caked on her windscreen and went to reverse out onto the track when a knock on her passenger window made her jump in fright.

Glenn, the cowboy with the movie star looks, smiled and waved as she wound down the window. 'Morning, shit, sorry did I scare you?'

Joanna's hand was over her heart. 'Scared the shit out of me, Jesus. Sorry I'm just a little jumpy after last night.'

'Totally understand,' he replied.

Joanna looked at his hands wrapped over the edge of the car door frame, his knuckles were scarred but surprisingly, his nails were clean. He just stared in through the windows at her with his piercing green eyes. 'So,' Joanna said awkwardly.

Glenn laughed. 'Sorry, ah, I was hoping for a favour? My ute's in town still, got a lift out with one of the boys. I was wondering if I could bum a lift?'

'Of course.' She thought it might be a good chance to feel him out. Ask him a few questions about the people from around here, try and get a better lay of the land from someone that wasn't her brother.

He jumped in and she noted he was still in his clothes from the night before. He'd showered, she could see his wet hair and he smelled faintly of Brut deodorant, but his jeans were still marked above the right knee with red dirt. Joanna indicated out onto the main road and set off towards town. The sun was still rising across the empty paddocks and she pulled down the visor in the car to mask her eyes from the blinding light.

'Beautiful, isn't it?' Glenn said after a few minutes of silence.

'It really is,' she replied.

'Benji told me a bit about you,' he added. 'Said you solved murders in the bush? He reckons your partner's that famous bloke who's on the telly all the time? Nick?'

'Vada,' she said, finishing his sentence.

'Yeah, Vada. Where's he now?'

Her mind briefly flashed back to the darkness, only for a split second, as she replied, 'Long story.' She didn't feel like getting into it so she changed the subject. 'Gabinda. Neville's based out of here? Is this where you all stay?'

Glenn nodded, as the brim of his Akubra just masked the stray rays of sun her visor wasn't catching. 'Pretty much our home base. Home base for all rodeo riding in the state. Nev's farm's like a school for bull riders and horseback riders. Got a big house and a big bunk house. Houses a heap of us. I spend spring and summers here. The rest I spend back home on the coast with my family. My parents are getting old.'

'The coast?' Joanna asked.

'Yeah, I'm from Ulladulla,' Glenn replied.

It was a long way away from where Joanna would have assumed he was from. The central coast of the state was full of beautiful coastal beach towns, and Ulladulla, near Batemans Bay was one of them. Set just over the Great Dividing Range on the coast behind sprawling rainforests, it wasn't a place she would assume a rough and tumble bull rider would come from. 'Yeah, right,' she replied. 'That's a long way from here.'

Glenn laughed. 'A long, long way. I still wonder sometimes how I got out here.'

Joanna looked ahead, it seemed like they were entering the Gabinda township. With a population of 6,000, Gabinda seemed to be the main hub for all the farmers in the region. The national highway narrowed and ran straight through it, and Joanna could see a long, space-age-looking caravan attached to a Nissan Patrol parked out front of a corrugated hut that had 'Gabinda Tourist Information Centre' above it. She continued on down and into the main street proper. On one side of the roundabout she'd entered was a decent-sized local supermarket. Beside that was a newsagent, a café, then a butcher shop. Further down she spotted a $2 shop, a hairdresser and another café. Gabinda seemed to have a bit going for it, she noted. Most small towns like this closer to Sydney were dead. Gabinda was not one of them.

Chapter Nine

She held the phone screen and tried to make sense of what she was seeing. All she could hear was screaming and laughter and then sometimes the dark stain of the redgum deck as the camera was held facing downwards, followed by a glimpse of the giant fan that spun slowly overhead in their rear entertaining area.

Jess Waterford, Nick Vada's sister, had told her husband Pete not to give the phone to their son, Tim, but the little toddler was relentless. He'd scream and cry if he wasn't allowed to hold the phone, and when he did, he'd be off like a shot out of a cannon, screaming and laughing like it was a game, as Pete tried in vain to catch their three-year-old son.

'Pete, Pete? Are you there?' she asked again into the receiver. 'I need to talk to you.'

She heard some complaining from her son and then suddenly the camera flipped up and her husband Pete was smiling back at her. His hair was a mess and his 'Waterford Grain' trucker hat balanced precariously on the top of his head. 'Hey. Sorry. He didn't nap today, apparently. Poor old Margie's only just left.'

Margie was an old family friend of Pete's mother, and had graciously offered to babysit their two kids when Jess raced to Morristown to be by her brother's side. Their daughter Sarah was nearing her first birthday and Jess's heart ached every minute she was away from her family. 'I'll text her after this. I know she doesn't want any money, Pete, but that woman's a godsend. If she won't give you her bank details, just jam some cash in her purse if you have to. I won't take no for an answer.'

Pete was a man of few words. From the moment they had met, Jess had taken the reins and run the show. She was an organiser, just like her brother. He was always compliant, he was a workhorse and a people person, and the main reason their farm 'Warranilla' had survived through a tough few years after everything that had happened.

'I'll sort it out,' Pete replied. 'I need to talk to you as well,' he added.

That sounded ominous, she thought. 'Why? What's up?'

She saw the base of a bottle of Great Northern beer as Pete took a swig, ready to muster the courage up to have the conversation she had honestly expected a week earlier. 'When are you coming home? I know what you're going to say, but it's almost been a month. If he's stable, you might need to just leave him for now.' He spoke fast, fearful that she was going to butt in. 'You can head back every weekend if need be. Totally up to you. I already spoke to Nigel Thomas about hiring his light plane. Get ya there in half the time. He owes me a few favours.'

Jess felt warm tears cascading down her cheeks. She sat in the family room next to the Intensive Care Unit of the Morristown Hospital. It felt like a second home to her by now. She could feel the groove she had made in the chair she sat in, the same chair she sat in every day when she couldn't sit and look at, or face her brother anymore. Sometimes she needed to get away for a short moment, even just to sit on her phone and scroll mindlessly for ten minutes, looking into the snapshots of her friends' lives that were continuing on with no worries in the world. It just wasn't fair. She knew she had to make the call herself, and had been having discussions with herself over the past few days, mustering up the courage to leave her older brother behind. His boss, Mark, and his partner, Joanna, had. She knew they were about as close to family as he was ever going to get and they were moving on with their lives.

She wiped the tears away on her cheeks and swiped her hair out of her eyes. 'I know. I know I need to make a call.' The tears came back. 'I just can't, Pete. I can't leave him here. He's all alone. I don't want him to be alone.'

'What about a transfer?' Pete asked. 'Get him back here? Milford Hospital? I could talk with Marianne's mum, she's a nurse there—'

Jess cut him off. 'He's too critical for that. He's in intensive care. If he's not here, he's in Sydney, and that's ten hours from where we are.'

Pete fell silent. 'Okay. I'm not sure what you want me to say.'

Jess looked up as Nick's doctor popped his head into the room and gave her a wave. 'Let's put a pin in this convo. Nick's doctor's here.'

'Alright,' Pete replied, she could hear the tone of defeat in his voice.

'I hear you,' she added. 'We'll talk more later.'

She placed her iPhone down on the arm of the worn lounge chair and watched as Nick's doctor walked over. He was tall and rake-thin, with clipped short hair and a dark goatee. He had been nothing but professional during Nick's stay in the hospital and

Jess had heard from a few of the nurses that he had come from a prestigious private hospital in Canada, one of the best in the northern hemisphere. She felt buoyed when she heard that. And it was a major reason why Nick remained where he was.

'You got a minute to speak?' he asked. His accent was formal and clipped at the end of each sentence.

'Of course.'

He sat down on the worn blue couch beside her, the same couch she had spread out across and slept on the first few nights of Nick's admission. He held an iPad in his hands, he was one of the only doctors she had seen that did so, and he opened up a file on it. 'Latest results from Nick's brain scans.'

She shifted in her seat. She had been waiting for two days for these results, they were the main thing keeping her there. 'And?'

'Good news. There's a marked improvement. Every marker has trended in a positive direction. The new drug we have trialled seems to be working.'

Jess felt like an enormous weight had lifted off her shoulders. The tears that had just stopped returned and she wiped them away quickly. 'That's great news! What does this mean? Does this mean he will wake up soon?'

The doctor was more tentative in his reply. 'Let's not get too excited. The brain scan is only one part of it. Consciousness, memory, gross and fine motor skills are the next big three that we need to be focusing on. Consciousness being the most important. When he wakes up, we will need to do a series of tests to ensure he's still the same brother you had as before. Something serious like this can affect some patients significantly.

When the doctor left, Jess made her way to the family bathroom and cleaned herself up, she wiped her face and re-tied her hair and then looked in the mirror: she looked like she'd been through the wringer. She thought bringing up her young kids had been hard, but this was a whole different level of physical and emotional torture. Satisfied she looked okay, she headed down the long hallway past the nurses' station.

Glenda, one of the head nurses, smiled warmly as she walked past. 'Good news, love?'

Jess held her hands up with her fingers crossed. 'Brain scans are getting better.'

'Great news,' she replied. 'I'll bring you a cuppa when I've got some spare time.'

Jess continued on, thankful of the nurse's kindness. Everyone had treated her like a member of a big extended family, and she was grateful for them now more than ever as she stepped over the threshold into her brother's room. The room was originally set for two patients, but was quickly reorganised just for Nick. He was now a hero in the area for helping solve the murder of one of their own local cops. Nick lay in the bed near the window, and she watched as heavy rain and wind lashed the glass from the outside. The bandage that had been around his head protecting the wound for the last few weeks had been taken off two days earlier and she had booked a local hairdresser who had come in and given him a haircut. Afterwards, she had spent the morning giving him his first shave.

She sat down in the leather chair beside him and watched as the tubes that ran into his nose gave him the extra oxygen he needed to stay alive. He had initially been on a respirator but it had been removed when his oxygen levels rose enough for him that they knew he could breathe on his own. She reached across and placed her hand on top of his. The news was getting better and better every day. She just prayed that when and if he woke, he'd be the same Nick she knew and loved.

'You can do it, Nick. I know you can.'

Chapter Ten

Joanna dropped Glenn off out the front of the local pub next to a shiny red Dodge Ram ute. Before he got out they had spoken a little more about their lives and their interests; Joanna felt the conversation was flowing well and she couldn't help but look at the veins tracking down his tanned forearm. She was attracted to him but didn't want to cause a fuss with her brother, it was one of his friends after all.

As he went to get out of the car he stopped and turned back to face her. 'You going to be in town for long?'

'No idea. I might need to help out if they can't find this little boy.'

Glenn chuckled. 'The young Blackwood? They'll find him. Gabinda's small. He can't have gone too far.'

Joanna hoped that was the case. She wasn't sure if she was truly ready to jump back into the deep end of a missing person's investigation. 'I hope so,' she replied.

'Thanks for the lift,' Glenn said. 'If you have any spare time, do you want to catch up for dinner? I'd love to get to know a bit more about you.'

Joanna smiled, they were on the same wavelength. 'Give me your phone.' He passed it over and she typed her number in and saved her name in there. 'Text me later, I'll let you know my movements.'

Glenn took his phone and gave her another tip of his hat. 'Appreciate it, thanks again.'

Joanna watched as he climbed into his car and started it. The loud drone of the V8 engine vibrated the rear-view mirror of her car. She watched as he turned a wide circle and then accelerated off into the distance. She felt the unfamiliar flutter of butterflies in her stomach and struggled to wipe the smile off her face. A guy like that in the middle of no-where, what were the chances?

Her phone rang and she read the name on the display on the dashboard: Jess Vada. She quickly answered. 'Morning.'

'Gee, you're up early, I thought I may have been leaving a message. Back at work yet?'

Jess sounded energised, Joanna could feel it. 'I'm not. I'm actually out of the city, a little excursion to see my brother. You sound happy, better? Good news I'm hoping?'

'Great news. I met with a doctor and he's got results for the latest brain scan. A marked improvement. All markers are trending upwards.'

'What does that mean for Nick? When will he wake up?'

'Too early to say. They are hoping to start lowering the dosages of sedatives they have him on. Doctors say that it's all up to him. Could be weeks, could be days, could even be hours.'

Joanna grinned. She suddenly felt lighter than she had in the last few weeks. She could see hope now. A future with her partner again. 'That's incredible. I just hope he's still him, Jess.'

There was silence for a beat. 'Me too,' Jess finally replied. 'I'll update you when I know more.'

Joanna hung up and sat in silence for a few short moments. It was good news. She needed it more than ever after the last few days she'd had. She breathed in and out of her nose for one minute and made a conscious effort to unclench her jaw. It was a technique she had learned recently in training, to try and calm herself. Initially she had thought it was stupid, but now she was finding herself doing it more and more. She indicated out of the dirt driveway in front of the pub and drove back down the main street, parking in front of the pale green coloured café that advertised 'The best coffee in town', and 'All day breakfast'. She was starving and needed some quiet time before she decided her next move.

She sat at a small table with her back to the wall, sipping on a latte. Most cafes in the last few years had upped their game, however, this place was not one of them. The young barista behind the machine had burnt the milk, and the coffee was bitter to the taste. *If this is the best coffee in town, Gabinda doesn't have good taste*, she thought.

She scrolled through Instagram on her phone and then placed it back down on her table when her breakfast came. She ate her poached eggs and avocado toast in silence, watching as people came and went, ordering their morning takeaway coffees and food, or sitting down to order. She wondered if they were speaking about the missing boy, or whether there was any news. She moved to pick up her phone - she wanted to call Benji for an update - when it vibrated in her hand.

Chief Inspector Mark Johnson was at the end of the line. 'Good morning, Detective.'

'Morning.'

'I hear you've taken a little holiday?' he asked. Joanna groaned. If he knew where she was that wasn't good news.

'I have. Come west to visit my brother. Just for a few days. Needed to get out of the city.'

'I get that,' Mark replied.

Joanna could feel an undertone in the conversation, like he was preparing to say something. 'Is there anything you need?'

'There is. I got a call from the Superintendent out at Dubbo late last night. He said you've got a missing person out there?' *There goes the holiday*, she thought. She knew what he was about to say before he even said it. 'Look, I know you wanted a break. But this might be just what the doctor ordered. Why don't you stay out at Gabinda for the week, give the local inspector and the local mob a hand, see if you can find this young bloke.'

'What about our cases?'

'Don't worry about them. Half of them have been re-assigned. With Nick out of action we had to. We need a senior lead on a lot of them and you're still green.'

Joanna didn't know whether to be offended or not but pushed past the comment. 'Alright. I'll take a look around. Give them a hand.'

'Good work. And if you need anything don't hesitate to call me.'

Joanna hung up and placed her phone back on the table. Matty Blackwood. Son of Gabby Blackwood. A potential heir to the Blackwood fortune. It seemed that John Blackwood was ready to move heaven and earth to get his grandson back. She suspected that by now if there had been no news, they could be looking for a body, but she knew to be more positive than that.

She paid for her breakfast, thanked the owner and headed out into the morning sun. The main street was busy for a Saturday morning, she assumed because in the bush most shops closed at lunchtime and weren't open Sunday, so people got whatever they needed on Saturday mornings. She got into her car and typed in Gabinda Police Station into her GPS. It was two blocks away. She drove over and parked in front of the small red-brick building. It was nestled between the primary school and a football oval. The wire fence out the front was tired and outdated, but the station looked like it had been blessed with the state government's last few rounds of grants. It looked modern and spacious, unlike most of the buildings in the small country town.

She walked through the front door into the front reception area and eyed a receptionist sitting at the front desk. She would have been in her sixties and had silver hair cut short with neat tortoiseshell brown glasses. She smiled warmly. 'Good morning, how can I help?'

Joanna walked up to the desk and placed her badge on the countertop. 'Detective Joanna Gray. I was hoping the Inspector was in?'

'Joanna,' she replied. 'We were just talking about you. Wondering when you would be here. I'm Julie. Nice to meet you.'

Joanna shook the woman's hand. She radiated a warmth and friendliness that she hadn't felt much in the rest of the town. 'Nice to meet you, Julie.'

'Inspector's office is at the back on the left.'

Joanna walked through the half height saloon doors into the open office space. There were five desks: two had people sitting at them and she could see the Inspector's office towards the back of the room. Sergeant Rossi stood up and walked over. 'Morning. I was hoping you'd come.'

Joanna smiled. She had liked the Sergeant the night before. She had a professional air to her that not all cops in remote areas had. 'Morning, Sergeant. Didn't have much choice. My boss called this morning.'

'Amelia, please,' she replied. 'Ah, yeah. Maybe my fault. I told Archie about you late last night. I told him you pulled us all into line and did a great job. I think he pulled a few strings.'

'It's okay. I was on leave anyway. I needed something like this to get me back on track. I met young Matty last night for a short moment. Seemed like a good young kid. I just can't understand where the hell he could have got to?'

'Yeah, it's a bit of a mystery. But we've got you now. Nick Vada's partner. You guys are the best of the best, I'm sure you'll find him in no time.' She pointed towards Archie's office. 'Inspector's office is there.'

Joanna walked past towards the office and suddenly felt the crushing weight of expectation. 'Nick Vada's partner', she had said. Suddenly she realised they must have an incredibly high opinion of her. Nick's name would do that. But she was a rookie, new to the detective game. She felt like an imposter.

She walked to the Inspector's office and knocked politely on the door. 'Come in,' he said.

The Inspector sat at his desk with a laptop off to the side. He was a small man, only a few inches taller than her and was balding aggressively. What hair he still valiantly held on to was diminished by the shining bald patch on top of his head. His nose was beetroot red, the sign of a heavy drinker. He stood up at Joanna's entrance, 'Good morning. Miss Gray, I take it?'

Joanna corrected him. 'Detective Joanna Gray.'

The Inspector shook her hand. His grip was surprisingly firm. 'Inspector Archie Zimmer. Please just call me Archie. Thank you for coming at such short notice.'

'It's no worries. It's the least I can do.'

'Sergeant Rossi said you took charge last night. She said you did a good job.'

Joanna blushed. 'Thanks. Just doing my bit. I met the young boy a few hours before he went missing. I can't believe how quickly things can go bad.'

'We haven't had many missing persons cases out here. In fact, in my twenty years here I can only think of two. And they were both sorted quickly. People were found quickly, usually still drunk from the night before, in someone's bed they shouldn't have been in. No lost kids though.' He waved the Sergeant to come in and she took a seat beside Joanna. 'I was hoping you and Sergeant Rossi could take the lead on this? Consider every officer in this station at your service. If you think things are getting more serious, I will speak to Cobar and ask for their missing persons team to help out. Let's hope we can find him sooner rather than later.'

'What can you tell me about the Blackwood family?' Joanna asked, and then went on to explain her awkward encounter with John Blackwood.

Chapter Eleven

His hearing had fully returned. It was his sister Jess's voice he recognised first. He listened as she spoke to him. Willing him to wake up, praying that he was okay. He listened as she spoke about life. About her husband Pete and her kids, Tim and baby Sarah. He smiled as she spoke about Tim and his penchant for breaking everything within sight. His love for his dad's motorbikes and the animals that all lived on the farm. He felt solace in the fact that their family would continue on after him and Jess were gone, and he felt sadness in realising that it may be too late for him now to start a family of his own.

He willed every fibre of his being to wake up. He felt like he stood behind a towering black wall, the door was right there, and every time he reached out to grab it, it would disappear into nothingness. Feeling slowly began to return to his body. He wasn't a vacant shape anymore. He felt his feet and toes come back first, he tried to wiggle them but the effort made him too tired. The warm sensation of feeling gradually rose up his legs and into his body, and then slowly into his arms and hands. He could feel the warmth of his sister's hand as it rested on his.

Senses began to return. He could feel the harsh plastic of the oxygen tubes that were still up his nose giving him oxygen. He could taste it at the back of his throat, the harshness of the medicines that were keeping him alive. Smell came next, he could smell his sister's perfume. He swore it was the one he had bought her for Christmas a few years back. A memory of standing in the shop and smelling the sample returned to him.

Sight was last. He pictured his eyelids, and willed every muscle he had in his body, to lift them up. He tried as hard as he could, and one time caught the faintest glimmer of white light. It was a good sign. He knew he could do it. He just had to rest now.

***

Archie spoke, 'The Blackwood family have been in Gabinda forever. Slowly over the last fifty to sixty years they've managed to buy up as much land as they could. They bought Riverleigh, the neighbouring farm about ten years ago, that made Moroco, their farm, one of the biggest in the state.'

'What do they farm?'

'Wheat, mostly. Yield-wise, they have one of the biggest wheat farms in Australia.'

'And there's good money in it?' Joanna felt out of her depth without Nick in her ear on these types of topics. This was his speciality.

'Millions. Wheat pricing at the moment is at a record high, and the Blackwood's have had quite a few good years.'

Joanna opened her iPad and began to type notes; it always helped her when she had a quiet moment to refer back to a single document. Nick was still working off paper and would always grumble at her use of technology. He was the oldest thirty-eight-year-old she'd ever met. 'Any updates since last night from the family?'

'Unfortunately not,' Amelia replied. 'I got off the phone with Gabby Blackwood first thing this morning. Nothing.'

Archie clicked his tongue. 'Hmm. The show will be packing up today, along with the rodeo. I've sent a group of local SES members to continue the search, along with Constable Webb. If he finds anything, he's been told to contact me straight away. We're going to need to get back there, ask around among all the vendors and workers. Surely someone somewhere has seen something.'

'What about Cameron Parsons?' Amelia said.

'Not Blackwood?' Joanna asked.

Archie shook his head. 'They aren't married.'

Joanna looked over at Amelia. 'What about him?'

'He's bad news. Always has been. Went with the bikies for a while when he was younger. We think he's still involved with drugs in the region, but never been able to pin much on him. He's got a mean streak that's for sure. Doesn't like coppers.'

Joanna's senses had been correct, she could feel something emanating from him the night before. 'He was okay with me last night,' she said.

'Putting on a straight face,' Archie replied. 'He's caused us problems in the past. We need to sniff around there, without upsetting Gabby, of course.'

Joanna and her new partner, Sergeant Amelia Rossi, walked back out into the sunshine and got into Amelia's four-wheel drive patrol car. 'Where to?' Amelia asked.

'Gabby Blackwood. Her house.'

'Done.'

Amelia spun the large car around and headed back towards the main street, went past the supermarket and turned left, heading away from the showgrounds. The roads were wide and the nature strips on the street were well-maintained. She turned down another street and Joanna noticed the level of care in home presentation dropping slightly. One lawn was yellowed and dying and one house had an old Commodore sitting in the driveway on blocks, slowly dripping oil and causing a giant stain. Ahead, Joanna could see a gaggle of cars parked near one residence that she assumed must be Gabby's. Amelia slowed to a stop and put the car in park.

Joanna's phone chimed and she read a text from her brother. *Where'd you get to?*

She tapped out a reply. *Helping the police look for Matty. Catch up later?* He liked her response, the small thumbs up making a dinging sound, and she placed her phone back in her pocket.

Joanna got out and eyed the house in front of her. It was not at all what she was expecting. The home was fibro, like the housing commission homes on the rough streets of the next suburb over from the one she grew up in. The gutter at the front dangled down off the fascia board, and the end of the sharp iron was precariously close to the front door. It looked like someone had begun to paint the home near the front main window, baby blue instead of the off-white it was, but had given up halfway through.

'Not what I was expecting,' Joanna said to Amelia.

The Sergeant shook her head. 'It's a long story. I'll explain later.'

They walked up the stairs to the front concrete porch and Joanna noticed a Bundaberg Rum can cut in half and full of cigarette butts. Joanna knocked on the metal security door and they heard bumping and scraping before the door opened. A woman around their age peered out, her eyes acclimatising to the bright sunlight. She smiled when she saw Amelia. 'Morning Sergeant.'

'Morning,' Amelia replied. 'Gabby here?'

'Sure,' she said, opening up the door. 'She's in the lounge.'

Joanna walked inside and ran her eyes around the room. It was messy but she could see signs of an attempted clean-up: bundled dirty clothes pushed into the corner of the lounge room, a child's toys stacked on top of a wooden chest. Gabby Blackwood sat at the small, round dining table with a cigarette in her hand and a mug of something hot sitting in front of her. She stood up suddenly when she saw them both. 'Oh my god! Do you have news?'

Joanna shook her head. 'I'm sorry. We don't.'

Gabby froze then slumped back down into the chair. She took a drag of her cigarette and let the smoke slowly drift out her nose. She looked like she had been crying all night, there were no tears left to cry. 'I just don't understand … Ice cream … The rides … Cameron … Where could he be? He couldn't have gone far.'

Joanna walked over and placed a hand on her shoulder. 'Gabby? Can I call you that?' Gabby nodded. 'Sergeant Rossi and I are here now. We are going to help.'

'Thank you. Benji texted me. He said you're the best of the best. Thank you so much for everything you have done so far. Dad said you would find him.'

Joanna flinched at the compliment. She said nothing in reply as Amelia asked, 'Is there anyone out there that you could think of who would want to hurt Matty? Or any reason why you think he could have run away?'

Gabby shook her head as big tears started to roll down her cheeks again. Joanna slid the tissue box on the table in her direction. 'No. Nothing. He's just a little kid, ya know? Wouldn't hurt a fly. He's quiet, always has been. Doesn't have too many friends at school, but we'd been working on that. Trying to get him into sport.' She laughed. 'He wasn't very good though.'

Joanna heard the screeching brakes of a car and the women all turned to the front window. The woman who had opened the door gave Gabby a look and then got up and walked outside. Joanna could just make out the shape of a man on the front footpath, who, going by his height, she guessed was Cameron. Heated words were being exchanged and thirty seconds later the front door flew open and Cameron stepped over the threshold. His face was flushed red with anger and he held a bottle of Jack Daniels in his hand.

'What the hell are you doing!' Gabby yelled. 'You're meant to be out looking for Matty!'

'What's the fuckin' point?' Cameron moaned. 'He's gone, Gab. And it's my fuckin' fault.'

Gabby stood up and walked over to the giant of a man who wrapped his arms around her delicate frame. Joanna watched Cameron intently. The man looked distraught, but if that was the case, why was he drinking and why wasn't he out looking for his son?

'Cameron, would you mind taking a seat? We'd like to ask you a few questions?'

Cameron seemed to finally notice the two police officers and his face turned sour. 'What are you lot fuckin' doin' in my house? Gab, I told you no coppers in the house.'

Gabby pushed him away. 'Cameron, they are here to help! Don't you understand?!'

'Just a few questions,' Joanna said. 'Please.'

Chapter Twelve

Joanna got back into Amelia's car, with more questions than answers. Amelia started the car, flicked the air conditioning on high and turned to her again, Joanna was ready. 'To the showgrounds,' she said.

Amelia indicated, and pulled out. Joanna asked, 'Alright. Cameron's story please.'

She took a deep breath. 'Fair enough. I've been here going on ten years now. Quiet place. All the usual dramas. Thefts on farms, car theft from time to time, domestic violence, public drunkenness, the odd fight at the pub. But nothing ever too serious. Cameron Parsons has always been bad news, he's given us trouble a few times over the years.'

'So, is he Matty's father?'

'As far as I'm aware, yes. Not my business to ask or know.'

As the car headed back into the more affluent area of town, Joanna asked the question she knew the Sergeant was waiting for. 'So, can you tell me why the hell Gabby Blackwood is with a guy like that? I don't understand. Richest family in the region and she's living in a house like that?'

'That is the million-dollar question. No-one really knows how or why the family had the falling out. Love does crazy things, I guess. Webby, the young constable, said the family don't talk at all anymore, not even her brother speaks with her,' Amelia replied.

'So, the whole Blackwood family are out on that big property and she's stuck here in town with a guy like him? I just don't get it. The Inspector said you think he's involved with drugs somehow in the region. Anything there?'

Amelia indicated towards the main street. 'Not really. We've seen him selling a little. We've searched him a few times; never found commercial quantities. Last time he was arrested I found him in the park in town near the war memorial completely out of it. Only thing I found on him was a couple of "pain pills", he called them. Nothing worth bothering anyone over.'

Joanna fell quiet, lost in thought. The young boy was gone, vanished without a trace and they had no idea why. She wondered if he could have been taken. Could there be something more sinister than all the hope that they are putting into the young boy just wandering off somewhere?

A phone ringing shattered the silence in the car and Amelia answered quickly. 'Hello.'

'Sarge it's Constable Webb. We found something.'

Joanna tensed in her seat. 'What is it?' she asked.

'His hat.' Constable Webb paused. 'We think.'

'Where are you?' Amelia asked.

'Behind the rodeo arena.'

Amelia hung up and accelerated towards the dirt road beside the local pool that led to the showgrounds. Joanna was the first person to speak. 'I'll be able to ID the hat. I saw him a few hours before he went missing.'

'Good,' she replied. 'I don't think Gabby's in a state to be coming down here for this. And there's no chance I'd ask Cameron.'

They reached the showgrounds quickly and Joanna noted that although the show and rodeo were over, only a few rides at the fairground had been packed up. The food vendor vans all remained as well, and some of them were open. Amelia pulled her police car around behind the rodeo arena and parked it close to the caravan of Benji's boss, Neville. As they got out, two men walked around the corner and Joanna realised it was Benji and Glenn.

'Afternoon,' Benji said to her.

'Hi. Sorry for running off this morning.'

'It's no worries; Glenn told me what you were up to anyway.' He pointed at Amelia. 'I had a feeling you'd end up giving them a hand. You well, Amelia?' he asked the Sergeant.

Amelia smiled. 'Wait a minute. Benji Gray? You're Joanna's brother?'

Benji laughed. 'What do you reckon, sis? I think you'll make a good detective out of her.'

Amelia punched Benji on the arm jovially. 'Ha ha. Very funny.'

Joanna's eyes had returned to the vans. 'Why is everybody still here? I thought the show people would be packing up and getting out of here?'

Benji shrugged. 'End of the season. Gabinda's the last show. Plus, it helps that most of the rodeo mob is from the region. The ride operators too. They start up north in Queensland and head their way down south as the season progresses.' He cleared his throat. 'A fair few have offered to help, you know? To look for Matty. We were out most of the night.'

Joanna had to commend her little brother. He was right. He hadn't got in until the early hours of the morning. 'And we thank you for that,' she replied.

'Have you seen Webby?' Amelia asked Benji.

Benji pointed to the stock crate trailer where Joanna had parked when she had first arrived. 'Last I saw, he was that way.'

'You got a minute?' she asked her brother. 'I might need a hand with something.'

The two men followed behind them as they made their way through all the parked utes. A crowd had formed near the bonnet of another four-wheel drive police vehicle, and the car door opened on their arrival. The young constable whom Joanna had met the night before, now had rubber evidence gloves on and held out a cap with the Chicago Bulls basketball team logo on it.

'That's Matty's,' Joanna said to the hushed group.

'Yep. She's right,' Benji added.

Joanna looked left and right. They were right on the edge of the dirt back road that she had come in on. She didn't need to say what she was thinking; as Amelia asked the constable, 'Any tyre tracks?'

He shrugged. 'Was windy last night. Have a look for yourself.'

The two women walked away from the group and down the table drain on to the road proper. Benji followed and knelt down near her. 'Four-wheel drive tyre tracks. Heaps of them though.' He pointed to a certain set of indentations. They're ATs. All terrain. Had them on one of my work utes once.'

'You can tell that?' Joanna asked.

'Sure,' he replied. He pointed further into the centre of the road. 'Hard to tell the rest though. Like he said, windy last night; washes everything away.'

Joanna took the information on board and walked on alone further down the track. She was lost in thought. Matty Blackwood, heir to the Blackwood family fortune, living in a fibro house in the rough end of town. Not a lot made sense. If someone had taken him, to what end? What did they stand to gain?

Amelia walked up behind. 'I'm not interrupting your process am I?'

'There's no magic process unfortunately. Information comes in. We figure out if it's viable, if not we push forward until the next snippet comes in.'

'What are you thinking?'

Joanna looked down where the dirt road connected onto the main highway where she'd entered. 'A few things. One: what did anyone stand to gain by taking him? And two: he could be anywhere. If he was taken by car, he could be halfway across the country by now.

The two women fell into a comfortable silence as they walked back to the expectant group. Joanna felt a little bit lost. She needed Nick with her to lead. He would have known what to do.

'Bag the hat. It'll have to be confirmed by Gabby just to be one hundred percent sure,' Joanna said to the Constable. 'C'mon, let's go interview the vendors, ask if they know anything else.'

The next few hours were fruitless. Joanna and Amelia walked down the row, questioning every person they came across, asking for more information. Joanna left her number with most, hoping that she would be contacted if some kernel of a memory popped back into their heads. Her phone pinged and she read a message from her brother. *We are headed to the pub. Dinner?*

'Let's call it for today,' she said to Amelia. She could see how tired the Sergeant looked. A case like this when you weren't making progress wasn't enjoyable for anyone. She tried to spy a wedding ring on her finger. 'You married?'

As they climbed back into the police car, Amelia laughed. 'No. Not a lot to choose from in Gabinda.'

Joanna thought about Glenn the cowboy. 'I don't know,' she replied. 'I don't mind the look of a few of those cowboys.' Amelia laughed and Joanna added, 'Want to join me and Benji at the pub for dinner?'

Amelia smiled. 'Alright. I didn't have anything else planned anyway.'

Chapter Thirteen

Night had fallen, and the room was pitch black dark around him and he was scared. He could feel how dry his tongue was and he needed a drink of water. He'd never liked water, he'd always complained to his mum that he wanted Fanta or cordial, but he didn't care at that moment. He needed something to quench his thirst. He knew to stay quiet, when he was quiet the bad man didn't come. He didn't want the bad man to come back, so he kept his hands over his mouth so no noise came out.

***

Joanna decided to not book a room at the pub. Something in the back of her mind told her to try something different for once. She wasn't sure whether it was because of what happened during her last pub stay, or whether she just craved more creature comforts than most old pub rooms had.

She checked into the Gabinda Inn, a twenty room, dark brown brick motel on the outskirts of town. Although the outside wasn't promising – gardens full of yellowed and dying weeds along with a large empty pool full of mould – the inside was much better than she'd expected. When the clerk advised her that the rooms had been recently renovated she didn't believe him, but when she entered the white, crisply painted room and fell onto the firm mattress, she was pleasantly surprised.

She quickly showered, changed into some lighter clothes and headed off to the pub. It was a short walk and she felt like a wine, or even a cider, something light to combat the heat of the day.

Her phone rang and she eyed the screen, she had called Hattie, her technical support analyst back at head office earlier in the day and requested she looked into Matty's phone data, to try and see if there were any anomalies. 'Any luck, Hattie?'

'Not a lot. It was switched off at 8:16 pm that night.'

That made sense, Joanna thought. That was around thirty minutes after Bryce the bull rider was injured. 'Anything else?'

'I've drilled down on a map layout of the showgrounds and the exact location it was turned off.'

'Let me guess. Right near Barnes Road?' Joanna had looked up the name of it earlier.

'Yeah, how'd you know?'

'Someone found his hat by the roadside. Must have come off when they were putting him into a car.'

'Jesus,' was all Hattie could say.

Joanna's brain ticked over. 'Social media. Is there any way you could check for any images around that night?'

'Sure,' Hattie replied. 'I can scrape socials with the hashtag Gabinda show or rodeo. I can also search any posts tagged at Gabinda that night. We have facial recognition software that could pick up his face from the crowd. Are you able to get some more photos of the young boy? The more we put into the software, the better it works.'

'Will do,' Joanna said. 'Thanks, Hattie.'

'Wait a sec. Any other news?'

Joanna didn't need to ask what she was talking about, she knew. 'About Nick? Brain scans over the last week are more positive. Trending in the right direction.'

Hattie sighed. 'God, I hope he's okay. I looked into the specialist who is treating him. He's one of the best in the world. So, we're lucky, I guess.'

Joanna chuckled. Looking into that sort of info was the exact type of thing she expected from Hattie. 'How's his record? Nothing we need to worry about.'

'He's clean, I checked,' Hattie replied, not picking up on Joanna's sarcasm. 'I'll call you soon.'

'Bye.'

The walk towards the pub wasn't long, but the late afternoon sun was still beating down and Joanna could feel it starting to burn her neck. She typed out a message to Mark to update him on her day, then placed her phone in her purse. She wanted to be present for her little brother.

Whoever did the gardens for the pub needed a raise, Joanna thought as she neared the pub. In front of the gravel carpark were rolling bright green lawns that were so freshly cut and manicured they almost looked like the astroturf you saw at a stadium. The pub itself had been tastefully renovated: it was about a metre off the ground and had a big deck out the front with a painted white balustrade. The roof was red corrugated iron and had the words 'Gabinda Hotel' painted across it in white.

Joanna eyed a red Dodge Ram in the carpark and tried not to smile. Glenn was easy on the eye and good conversation, and she wasn't averse to having her mind taken off her last month.

Benji's head popped up over the railing. 'Oi!'

'Oi yourself,' Joanna replied.

She walked up the timber ramp. Bench seats were spread out underneath the pergola and ceiling fans tried in vain to circulate the warm soupy air. She looked up and felt a tickle of mist down her back and spotted the black hoses connected to the misting fans.

'Mist alright?' Benji asked, pointing up to the fans. 'Some chicks don't like it messing with their make-up.'

Joanna saw Glenn already sitting at the table with Amelia and smiled at her brother. The make-up she used to cover the burn scars across her face was so thick it was almost waterproof. A bit of mist wouldn't hurt it. 'Do I look like someone who'd be bothered by a bit of mist?'

Benji laughed. 'Alright, fair enough. What do ya want to drink?'

'Cider or a white wine is fine. Any updates on Bryce? How is he?'

Benji grinned. 'Better than what we first thought. The horn cut that big hole in his chin but hasn't done any serious damage. His throat and voice box are all intact still, so that's a win. Didn't hit any major tendons either, knocked his bottom row of teeth loose pretty bad, that's what's causing him the most pain. His old man has travelled to be with him for a few nights. He avoided any major surgeries.'

Joanna's mind flashed back to that night, the image of the hole in his chin would be etched in her mind forever. 'Well, let's hope he's okay,' she replied.

Benji left her to head off and order. She walked over to the pair at the table and watched Glenn's green eyes slowly look at her and then run down her body and back up again. He smiled at her, he seemed to like what he saw. She moved in close and slid along the seat beside him. 'Afternoon,' she said to them both. 'Hasn't cooled down yet.'

'Nah,' Glenn replied. 'Won't til the sun goes down.'

When Benji returned the four fell into easy conversation. Amelia talked about her time in Gabinda and how the Inspector was nearing the end of his career. Her plan was to take over the reins from him in the new year. Glenn spoke of bull riding, and his love of animals. Joanna watched him intently. He was good-natured, kind and extremely passionate about those topics.

Lastly, she watched Benji as he explained his last year and how he was learning to become a bull rider. Joanna was sad to think about the many years she had missed out on seeing her little brother grow up but was proud of the man he had become.

As day turned into night, the group ate dinner and then headed into the pool area for a few games. The crowd slowly built and Amelia and Benji would stop from time to time and point out a face, and explain who they were and any relevance to a case. Joanna had to laugh; although she knew her partner Nick was a borderline alcoholic, his idea of heading to the pub in all these towns had usually turned out to be invaluable.

A tall man in a bone-coloured Akubra cowboy hat walked in with a brunette and sat down at the bar with a group of friends. 'That's Casey Blackwood,' Amelia said, pointing in his direction. 'He was at the showgrounds helping us look.'

'What's his story?' Joanna asked.

'John Blackwood's only son. Private school kid. Come back to run the family farm. Heir to Moroco. He's a straight shooter. A bit of a mean bugger, short with conversation. Just like his dad.'

As Benji spoke, Casey turned and spotted the group at the pool table. He spoke shortly to the woman and then headed in their direction. 'Evening. Shouldn't you all be out looking for my nephew?'

You've seen one, you've seen them all, Joanna thought when she looked at his smug smile. Rich farmers. They always thought they ran their respective towns. They always thought they were above the law. 'Shouldn't you?' Joanna snapped back.

Casey blinked and then smirked. 'Fair call.' He leaned on the edge of the pool table. 'I'm guessing you're the Sydney detective Dad was talking about. Any updates?'

Amelia and Constable Webb had taken the cap around to Gabby who confirmed it to be Matty's. Amelia had told Joanna that Gabby was taken aback, and confused as to how it could have got there. Joanna thought that seeing the hat, and the police explaining the meaning of it being next to a dirt road connected to a highway must have made things a lot more real for the woman.

'Detective Joanna Gray,' she answered. 'We found his cap. On the edge of Barnes Road, right near the truck parking area behind the rodeo arena.'

Casey nodded. 'I heard. Dad's got two of our workers out that way tonight, scouring the sides of the road, to see if they can find anything else.'

Joanna stood firm. 'And if they found anything they'd be reporting it straight back to us, of course?'

'Of course.' He turned back towards his friends. 'Well nice meeting you. If you need anything from me, don't hesitate to ask. Have a good night.'

He turned back and headed to his group of friends. He shot a quick look back at Joanna who kept her eye on him. Just as he reached his group a hush fell quickly over the bar, as Cameron Parsons stumbled inside. He still held the same bottle of Jack Daniels in his hand that he had during the afternoon, but now it was empty. Joanna looked at Amelia and nodded. Simple words unspoken between the two cops. *Let's sort this out before it explodes.*

Cameron had propped up on a stool at an awkward angle and sipped on a beer. His eyes were straight down in his glass and as they both walked over Amelia cleared her throat as she got to him. 'Uh-erm.'

Cameron spun around, almost teetering off the barstool. 'Whadda you lot want?' he slurred.

Amelia edged in closer as the crowd had fallen quiet again, eagerly trying to listen in to their conversation. 'Cameron. Mate. Don't you think you've had enough? Are you sure you should be here? You should be home with Gabby right now. Being there for her.'

Cameron exploded up out of the stool and Amelia took a fast step back. 'You can't fuckin' tell me what to do! Why don't you lot just fuck off!'

Joanna stepped forward, she wasn't going to be bullied by a drunk. 'Mr Parsons. We aren't going to ask again. If you need us to call the station, we'll have a truck here in a few minutes.'

Cameron spat on the floor at her feet. 'Fat lot of help you've been! Meant to be the fuckin' star, they say! I call bullshit!'

Benji and Glenn joined the group and Benji shouted loud enough for everyone to hear. 'Oi, Cameron, if you don't get out of here, we're going to carry you out, mate.'

Cameron stuck his tongue out at them and started laughing, a manic, crazed laugh that filled the bar as he turned and walked away. 'Cops. Bloody good lotta help they are.' He was still talking to himself as he stumbled out the front door into the darkness.

Joanna turned back to Benji. 'I can fight my own fights, little brother.'

Chapter Fourteen

Joanna finished her round of pool and her drink and wished everyone goodnight. She could see the disappointment in Glenn's eyes but while Benji and Amelia were in conversation she told him they should catch up for dinner again soon. That had seemed to make him happy. She was tired and her social battery was running low. She needed to be alone with her thoughts and being in the noisy pub wasn't helping.

Her walk back to the motel was uneventful and she used the quiet peace to try and put together the last day's events chronologically and figure out just what could have happened to the young boy.

She had turned the air conditioner on to its highest setting before she left, and when she walked back into her room, it felt like a freezer. Just the way she liked it. She stripped off and took a quick cool shower, placed on some of the facial healing cream that she used on her burn scars overnight, placed her phone on the charger with no alarm, lay down and fell into a deep sleep almost immediately.

The next morning she woke at 7:00 am on the dot. As she got older her body clock seemed attuned to that time and she never tried to sleep in. She slid out of bed and, although she didn't feel like it, put a thirty-minute yoga routine on her phone. She got down on the floor and stretched herself into all sorts of positions she was never fully prepared for, feeling her muscles and joints welcome the deep stretching, it was how she tried to start every morning.

She stopped past the coffee shop on her way to the station and picked up some takeaway coffees. She knew that in a police station this far out, that orders wouldn't be too crazy and took a stab in the dark with what everyone would want. She ordered two lattes, two cappuccinos and one long black. There was always someone in the group who had to tell you about their long blacks.

The station seemed busy, and there were more cars parked out the front than the day before as she made her way inside. Julie, the receptionist was propped up in her same spot. 'Morning Detective, what have we here?'

Joanna held up the carry tray and paper bag. 'I come bearing gifts. What sort of coffee do you like?'

'Got a cappuccino?' she asked.

Joanna handed one of the cups over. 'Of course.' One down, she thought.

Inside, Amelia sat with Constable Webb at one of the desks. Joanna could see a Berocca sizzling in a glass beside her elbow. 'Morning.'

'Morning,' Amelia replied as she pointed to the tray. 'One of them isn't for me, I suppose?'

'What would you like?'

'Got a latte?'

'I do,' she said.

Joanna looked over at the Inspector's office and could see the back of someone sitting across from him. 'Who's that?' she asked.

'John Blackwood,' Constable Webb replied. 'Don't have a cappuccino there as well?'

Joanna handed her second last coffee over. Right again. 'Yep, here you go. I'm going to see what this is all about.'

'Good luck,' Amelia said.

She walked over towards the office after leaving the pastries with the two hungry cops and rapped her knuckles lightly on the glass. 'Morning. Coffee?'

John Blackwood turned around at her entrance. He was red in the face. The Inspector seemed happy about the intrusion and stood up. 'Detective Gray you're here! Thank you. Don't suppose you have a long black? It's all I drink, I don't know how people can drink milk with their coffees; kills the flavour.'

She handed the final coffee over. She was getting good at this. 'Here you go.'

The Inspector took the coffee and drank from it immediately as John Blackwood continued. 'As I was saying before, what are we doing here? You've got two locals and yourself, plus her,' he said pointing at Joanna like she wasn't even in the room. 'Where's the helicopters? Where's an army of cops?' His voice rose as he made each point. 'My grandson is out there somewhere, Inspector! And you're here having coffees! Doing fuck all!'

Joanna cut in, the Inspector didn't look like much of a fighter and he looked like he'd shrunk a foot in his chair. 'Yelling at us isn't going to help the process, Mr Blackwood.' John opened his mouth to retort but she pushed on. 'And I'll have you know, we are doing our best. We've still got the SES and the team out there looking. We've found his hat on the edge of Barnes Road, which means that there is a high likelihood he's been taken off site. Day three is crucial and there are many things we have on our list to do. So, with you here taking up all of our time, we can't progress in any way.'

John Blackwood looked like he wanted to continue the argument, but the momentum he'd had before she'd walked in seemed to have gone. The redness in his face began to leave it. 'Alright, alright. Fair enough.'

She took a seat down beside him as the Inspector mouthed a thank you. 'Now as I said, day three is crucial. Sergeant Rossi is going to be spending the day reviewing the evidence we have, which sadly isn't much right now. We've asked any vendors at the showgrounds who had CCTV to submit it and we've had some in overnight. Also, I have my tech team in Sydney trawling all social media, we have quite good facial recognition software so if young Matty is in any images, we'll know about it.'

John seemed taken aback. 'Alright then. Well, it sounds like you're on it.'

She smiled her sweetest smile. 'I am.' John moved to get up and she continued. 'Before you go. I've been asking everybody this. Is there absolutely anyone you know of that had it in for Matty, or Gabby and Cameron?'

John scoffed. 'No. But my son-in-law Cameron, that's a different story. Bloke is a druggie. Whole town knows that. If Matty's been taken by anyone, that'll be why. Probably owes someone money for drugs or something.'

'And how do you know that?' Joanna asked.

John shrugged. 'Bloke hasn't worked a day in his life. Tried to bring him out to the farm a few times and he lasted a few hours. Lazy prick.'

'Being lazy doesn't make you a drug dealer,' Joanna retorted.

'I've heard things,' John said. 'Enough to convince me.'

'Anybody else?' Joanna asked.

'What about Carl Luvici?' John said in the Inspector's direction.

The Inspector rolled his eyes. 'It's been twenty odd years John. Carl's been a stand-up citizen ever since.'

'Who's Carl Luvici?' Joanna asked.

'A bloody kiddie fiddler,' John replied. 'That's what he is. Got locked up for years and then got out. Now he's back here. You should never have let him back in the town,' he added in Archie's direction.

That's interesting, Joanna thought. Any person involved with children that was on the sex offenders register would always raise red flags. 'We'll bring him in for a chat anyway,' Joanna replied to John. 'If he is what you say he is, he's worth talking to.'

John Blackwood left shortly after and Archie thanked Joanna for saving him, those were his words. She wondered how he made it to Inspector while being so spineless. Most inspectors she'd met in her time were tough as nails, no nonsense types. Now she knew why Amelia thought she could run the station at Gabinda.

Joanna left Amelia and Constable Webb alone as they reviewed all the CCTV footage. She got into her car and headed back to the showgrounds where the SES had set up a small command station overnight, to help keep the searchers organised, fed and hydrated. She spoke with the head of the search team and told him they were expanding the search to a thirty-kilometre radius, which would have to be done by cars if the members of the SES were okay with that. The showgrounds and rodeo area, along with the carpark, had been searched, and besides Matty's hat, nothing had been found.

She called Amelia as she got back into her car. 'Any luck?'

'Nothing as of yet,' Amelia replied. 'Most of these cameras are junk. Black and white. Can't see much.'

'Keep looking.' Joanna had done her fair share of poring over CCTV footage. Sometimes, with a little patience, you could find gold. 'What do you know about a Carl Luvici?'

Amelia chuckled. 'Oh god. Luvici? Owns the local florist. Went to prison back in the 1980s for paedophilia, inappropriate touching of a minor. Got out in the 90s. We haven't had any bother out of him. I knew his name would come up. Did John Blackwood say something?'

'He told us we need to look into it,' Joanna replied.

Amelia laughed. 'This town sometimes, I swear. You know what it's like. Whenever anything happens untoward, he's the first name that comes to mind.'

Joanna understood that. Even back in Milford there were the select few names that were brought up whenever any law was broken. Rural policing was sometimes easier than the big city as the suspect pool was always pretty thin.

Amelia gave her his home address. As she got closer, she realised it was the building his florist shop was in; she assumed he had a small flat at the back. The building was new and tastefully designed. Brilliant blooms of flowers filled every corner of the building. As she walked in through the front door, a bell chimed and a voice yelled out, 'Coming!'

A man popped around the corner from down a hallway wearing maroon corduroy pants and a horizontal black and white striped shirt. He wore a blue beret and Joanna could see why people in the town felt uncomfortable, the man had a very eccentric fashion sense that would've been abrasive to the locals in the bush.

His smile at Joanna turned into a curious expression. 'You're that detective, aren't you?'

'How'd you know?' she asked.

He shrugged. 'Whole town's talking. Plus, I expected I'd be seeing you soon enough. Anything goes wrong with kids and I'm mentioned. A kid goes missing and the whole town would be pointing at me.'

Joanna almost felt sorry for him, but remembered his criminal record. It didn't matter to her that it had been thirty years ago. Most offenders never grew out of those sorts of things. 'Well then, you'd understand if I asked whether you were at the Gabinda Show on Friday night?'

He placed the bunch of flowers he held in his hands and opened his phone up. He went into his gallery and opened up a photo, turning the phone in her direction. In the images, he stood with three other flamboyantly dressed men at what looked to be a men's cabaret bar. 'I was in Sydney. Only got back this morning. Happy for you to call any of the men in this image to corroborate.' *A dead end,* Joanna thought. 'While you're at it, feel free to search for any missing children out the back.'

Joanna smiled. A barb in her direction. She probably deserved it, he sounded like he was used to being hassled, but she wasn't bothered. A child was missing, and the boy was what mattered the most. She didn't care about his feelings.

She left the florist shop and Carl closed the door and locked it behind her. He gave her a sour smile as he flipped the closed sign around. As she walked back to her car her phone rang. Jess Vada was calling again. 'Hello? Everything okay?'

'Jo. He's awake!'

Chapter Fifteen

Nick was back in Milford again, or was he? He stood at the entrance of the caravan park, where the bitumen road turned to dirt near the boat ramp and looked over at the body of water.

How did he get here? He couldn't remember. He looked down at what he was wearing. Board shorts, thongs and a t-shirt. It was hot. *Must have been heading that way for a swim*, he thought; no point in turning away now.

He walked slowly down the dirt road towards the edge of the river, feeling the heat off the road radiating up at him. The river was busy. There were water ski boats parked on the small beach; he counted five. He watched as one slowly motored away towing a ski biscuit. He couldn't really think of another place he'd rather be in the world as he kicked his thongs off close to the river and pulled his t-shirt off up over his head. The sand close to the dark water was cool on his feet, a welcome reprieve from the heat, and he slowly walked into the lukewarm water. He got to his waist, and then, mentally preparing for the blast of cool, he closed his eyes and jumped in.

***

His eyes opened slowly and he blinked a few times, trying to acclimatise to the abrupt brightness. He wasn't in the river anymore that was for sure, and his body felt like it weighed a tonne. A figure sitting in a chair by his side slowly became clearer and he smiled when he realised it was his sister, Jess. She was engrossed in her phone and by the looks of her face was dead tired. It looked to be night time outside and he wondered how long he'd been out for.

'Evening,' he said slowly to her. The word felt slow, like it had just rolled out of his mouth.

Jess's head flicked up. 'Nick?'

'Hey.'

Jess shot up out of the chair in excitement. 'Oh my god!' She ran to the call button. 'Kathy!' She turned back to him, her face showing astonishment. Tears burst out of her eyes and he watched as she patted his arm. 'You're okay!' she said. 'You're alive!'

'Of course I'm okay,' he said. He wondered how long he was out for. Was he swimming back at Milford? Or was that a dream? 'Where am I?' he asked.

'Morristown,' she replied. 'In the intensive care unit.'

He knew Morristown. It was in the state's south. Near the Great Dividing Range, a mountain town. 'Morristown? How'd I get here?'

'It's a long story,' she replied. She sat down and slid her chair close to him, and placed her hand on his. 'You've been in a coma, Nick. There was an accident. Joanna saved your life.'

Nick felt his mind slowly trying to recalibrate as he heard the words. Morristown. Coma. Accident. Joanna. He must have been on a case here, he realised. 'Joanna,' he asked. 'Is she okay?'

Jess smiled. 'She is. She'll be so happy to hear you're okay.'

'How long was I out?'

Jess's smile vanished as she looked towards the door. 'Perhaps we should wait for a doctor?'

Nick pressed his hands down and tried to slide further upright in the bed. His whole upper body felt like it was numb, his arms looked like they had lost muscle, and he could feel that he had lost weight. 'Just tell me, Jess.'

Jess could sense the seriousness in his tone. 'Nearly six weeks.'

Six weeks. His mind couldn't comprehend it. He tried to think about how he had come this far south of the state and why he was here. He said nothing, unsure what he was supposed to do with the information. His mind reeled. It couldn't pinpoint anything in his past correctly. He thought back hard. He remembered that he was a detective. He remembered his father's death. He remembered who killed his mother. He remembered the Belle Smith case. The face of his partner Bec floated back into his memory. 'Bec?' he asked looking at Jess.

'Bec? She's engaged now, Nick, remember?'

An engagement? He couldn't remember, he watched his sister warily. 'Of course,' he replied. He didn't want her to know how confused he was. He wanted to get out as soon as possible.

A doctor and nurse arrived and gave him a short assessment. They were shocked he had woken up so soon but told them both to be wary, sometimes coma patients could slip in and out, so they dimmed the lights and left him alone with Jess. He could tell they'd bumped his medication up, and he felt himself slowly drifting away again, this time to sleep.

The next morning, the doctor and nurses returned and this time spent the next few hours doing tests. They checked his pupils to see whether they reacted correctly to the lights; motor responses and reflexes in his limbs; and then finally the big one, a cognitive assessment. The doctor and nurse went through a list of questions and he did his best to answer them, while Jess watched on warily.

When the doctor finished, he spoke candidly to Nick. 'You're in a lot better shape than I thought you would be, Nick. Just because you're awake doesn't mean that you're fixed though. This recovery is going to take time. Firstly, we are going to need to do some further brain scans to see what damage this coma could have done to it. You may need medication to help ease some of the swelling there still and level out some emotional responses. We will need to do some physical therapy, you may not realise it, but you've been in this bed for six weeks, and most of the muscles in your legs will be wasted, we will need to teach you how to walk again. Lastly, psychological care. You've been through something highly traumatic. I think, going by your cognitive assessment, that you have some short-term memory loss. Now, knowing your profession, I'm sure you don't want to admit that.'

'My memory is fine,' he replied as his sister rolled her eyes.

When the doctors left, a rehab nurse came in and introduced himself as Byron. He was a tall man with a big, red bushy beard and cheery demeanour. He didn't waste any time and quickly had Nick's legs dangling off the edge of the bed. 'Alright, big shot. Doc said you're talking a big game. He reckons you may be walking out of here any moment.'

Nick smirked, buoyed by the challenge as Jess watched on with a worried look. 'Let's see how I go.'

He pushed himself off the bed and felt Byron's strength as the nurse supported ninety percent of his body weight. The lower half of his body felt dead, he could hardly feel his feet, but as the blood in his body started to circulate again, with Byron's assistance, he managed to make it to his door and back before collapsing on the bed in a sweaty mess.

A few hours later, he sat upright in his bed and ate his first proper meal since he woke. It was a chicken sandwich, and one of the best he had ever had, he thought, as he struggled to hold the weight of it up to his mouth. Jess filled him in, as much as his boss, the Chief Inspector had allowed, before he could do a proper debrief, and Nick was starting to feel like himself again.

He wasn't sure what it was, but he felt her presence nearby before he saw her. Jess must have seen her first because she burst into tears, and he turned to see his partner, Joanna, walk into the room. 'Nick,' she said as tears ran down her face. She walked up quickly, nearly knocking his lunch off the hospital table, and fell onto him and wrapped her arms around him. 'I thought you were dead,' she said into his shoulder.

She got up slowly, and he looked at his partner up close for what felt like the first time. She looked tired, and the vibrant energy that always drove her, looked like it had been worn away slightly. He could still feel it there, but it felt dulled. He smiled and realised that he too was crying. He was just glad she was safe. 'Nah. They haven't got me yet,' he said.

She laughed, wiping the tears away. 'Good to see you still have your sense of humour.'

Behind her, his boss and mentor, Chief Inspector Mark Johnson, strolled in. He was in full dress uniform and held a thick leather binder. He took off his hat at the sight of Nick, and grinned. 'Took you long enough.'

Nick smiled back at his boss. He wasn't one for pleasantries. 'Nice of you to dress up for me. Sorry for sleeping on the job.'

Jess left the three cops and headed off to begin packing up to return home. Joanna snuck in some chocolate from the vending machine and a can of Coke No Sugar, and he drank the fizzy drink slowly, while feeling the sugar from the chocolate immediately make him feel a little better. The Chief's tone was more serious. He explained why he was in the hospital and what had happened in Blarnie afterwards. Nick tried to rack his mind for anything that could make him remember but it just wasn't coming to him. He made a point to be vague in his responses; he didn't want the Chief to get a gauge on his memory loss.

When the Chief was done, the trio fell into momentary silence. Nick asked. 'So, what's next for me?'

The Chief sipped from his coffee cup. 'Let's just focus on your recovery, mate. For now, let's get you back on your feet. You're on sick leave, full pay, for as long as you need it. There was no pushback from up above on that. You're a hero in our office as far as we're all concerned.'

Chapter Sixteen

When Joanna heard the news, she had raced back to the motel room and packed up her small bag. The Chief had booked her a regional flight out of Cobar and she had held on for grim life in the small twin-engine plane all the way to her connecting flight in Dubbo.

Once in Dubbo she hired a car and raced to Morristown, buoyed by the fact her partner was awake. She had been hoping and praying the day would come, and now that it finally had, she felt mixed emotions. She was still angry at him for going off alone and putting himself in such danger, but she didn't want to voice her opinion just yet; she didn't know how bad his injury was.

As she pulled into the Morristown hospital car park, she saw the Chief Inspector speaking with someone on the footpath. He was wearing his full dress uniform, which was odd and she asked him about it when she walked up to him. 'What's the occasion?'

He rolled his eyes. 'New station just opened in Englefield, down the road. Nick timed it perfectly, I was only an hour away.'

Joanna laughed. 'Station openings? Really? What, are you gunning for the Superintendent job?'

'The pay wouldn't be bad,' he replied. 'But I like my band of misfits in Homicide. You're stuck with me for a while yet, unfortunately.'

As they walked towards the hospital doors, her phone rang and she looked at the name on the screen. Sergeant Amelia Rossi. She wanted to see Nick, but wondered what news she might have.

'Afternoon.'

'Hey Joanna. You got a second?'

Her tone sounded serious, she mouthed to the Chief Inspector to give her a minute and he walked onward through the hospital doors. 'What is it?'

'It's Cameron Parsons. He's missing.'

Joanna looked up at the cloudless sky and closed her eyes. What more could go wrong? 'Missing? You sure? He's probably somewhere sleeping off that bottle of Jack Daniels.'

Amelia sounded tentative. 'I don't know. We've had Gabby Blackwood in here this morning. She's beside herself with worry. First Matty and now Cameron. She says that no matter how much he drinks, no matter what he gets up to he always manages to make it home. His phone's off and she hasn't heard a word. God, I hope it's not connected to Matty in any way.'

A terrible thought popped into Joanna's head. 'What if he's with Matty?' she asked.

'The Inspector said the same thing. I don't know. What do you think?'

Joanna thought for a second. Cameron seemed extremely hurt at the pub. Although that didn't mean anything, she had seen many guilty people act the same way. 'I don't know. Look, I've got to go. Give me an update later on today if he's shown up or not. I don't know what my boss has planned for me. Whether he wants me back out there or not. I'll keep you posted.' Joanna hung up and took a breath in preparation to walk in and face her partner.

She hadn't known what she was expecting, but, he had looked different to her. Thinner, rougher, with a glaze to his blue eyes she'd never seen before. She watched him closely as the Chief Inspector explained to him just how close he'd been to losing his life. He listened, chimed in from time to time, but to her, something was missing. She just couldn't put her finger on it.

The Chief continued to speak, updating him on some of the other cases that their team was working on and she excused herself to get another coffee. As she walked to the tearoom near the nurses' station she ran into Jess, who was sitting in a well-worn chair in the corner of the room. She looked up from her phone. Joanna could see how worn out she was, how tired, and hoped that now Nick was awake she could rest.

'He looks better than what I thought he would,' she said in Jess' direction. She wasn't sure why she said that.

Jess had a sad expression. 'He does. I was so scared. I wasn't sure if he was ever going to come back.'

Joanna neglected finishing making her coffee and sat down beside Jess, placing her hand on hers. 'He's going to be okay, Jess.'

Jess explained about the cognitive tests, and her worry about him jumping straight back into work. 'It's his life, Jo. I know that. I just get so worried about him. He only has you. I feel like sometimes he thinks he has nothing to lose. He has everything to lose, he has you, he has a family. He's an uncle now. I want my kids to grow up with him in their lives.'

'They will, I promise you,' Joanna replied, although she wasn't sure whether she should be making that promise.

She finished making her coffee and headed back to the room. The Chief Inspector was outside in the hallway, deeply engrossed in a phone call and she walked into the room again to see Nick staring wistfully out the window. He turned to her and smiled. It was a joyous one that spread from his lips and then right up to his eyes. When the smile came she saw the faintest glimmer of spark that he had always had.

'How are you feeling? Really?' she asked him as she sat on the edge of the bed.

Nick shrugged. 'Better than I properly should.'

Joanna watched him closely. He was being guarded, she could tell. 'But ...'

'But?'

'Something's up. I can see it in your eyes.'

'Nothing's up, Joanna. I promise.'

Whatever it was, it could wait, she thought. 'Well while the Chief's out of the room, want to do a little policing?'

She outlined her last week, her trip to Gabinda, the rodeo, Gabby Blackwood, Matty Blackwood's disappearance, the hat, the road and finally now Cameron Parsons' apparent disappearance. Nick sat quietly and didn't interrupt, seemingly taking all the information on board until she fell silent.

'What's Gabby Blackwood's story?' he asked finally. 'You've been told about her partner, how he's bad news. Seems like this Blackwood family has a bit of history between the dad and siblings. Might be worth digging into that.'

Joanna nodded. It was a fair point. She hadn't thought much about Gabby because she had been with her on the arena floor at the time the boy had gone missing.

Nick continued. 'What about Hattie? I'd get her looking into his phone. Scrape it. Scrape social media, she has this new facial recognition software. Try that.'

'Done all of that already,' Joanna replied.

Nick smiled and patted her on the hand. 'Sounds like I taught you well then.'

She looked into his bloodshot eyes. 'You really want to keep doing this?' She pointed at the monitors beside him. 'After all of this?'

'It's my life, Jo. What else have I got?'

After discussing some more of her ideas about the case, Joanna headed out to find the Chief. He was still on a call and she waited until he hung up. The Chief pointed to Nick's room. 'So, what do you think?'

She'd had a few hours with him now. Although he wasn't fully back, and she sensed something wasn't quite right, it was still Nick. She knew that he would come good. She was sure of it. 'He just needs time. Needs time to heal, to rest.'

The Chief sighed. 'The commissioner asked me if I think I should promote him. Give him a desk job. Based in Sydney.' He rubbed his eyes, out of frustration Joanna assumed. 'What do you think I should do?'

Joanna pointed back towards the doorway. 'Chaining that man to a desk would be worse than a life sentence. He'd be out of the force within months. He loves what he does, and he's good at it.'

'Pretty much word for word what I said to the commissioner. Good to see we are on the same page.'

'What do you want me to do?' Joanna asked.

'If you want to head back to Gabinda to keep looking around, do it. I don't want you working on anything new until Nick is ready to return, if he wants to. Once he's made the call, you can decide what you want to do.'

Joanna nodded. She wanted to finish what she had started out there. She didn't want to pick up anything new in the city either. And most of all, she wasn't ready to lose Nick as a partner just yet. She headed back into his room and explained what she was going to do. Nick seemed hesitant to see her go, but wished her good luck, and told her to call him or message him any time she needed help. She left the hospital feeling prepared for whatever she was going to find in Gabinda.

Back at the Dubbo airport she dropped off her hire car and mentally prepared for the small plane trip back to Cobar. As the single engine propeller plane taxied towards the runway where she was going to get in, Hattie rang.

'Hey Hattie. I don't have long, sorry, about to get on a flight.'

'Hey Jo, sorry, I'll make it quick. I was just checking in on Matty Blackwood's phone. Trying to go through his last hour's movements again when I realised it had come back online.'

Joanna nearly dropped her phone. 'Online? Where?'

Chapter Seventeen

Casey Blackwood watched Cameron Parsons closely. Cameron had stormed into the pub with a bottle of Jack Daniels in one hand and got into a screaming match with the local Sergeant and the Sydney Detective. As Casey had walked back out of the pub and into the night, an idea formed in his head, solid and immovable.

That afternoon his father had called a meeting. He wanted everyone at the house, no matter what. Casey had pulled up with his wife, Tori, and spotted a rare sight. Under the shade of the gum trees that lined the west side of the house beside the water tank was his sister's battered old Toyota Corolla.

'This'll be interesting,' he said to his wife. His sister hadn't been home to the farm in years. Casey couldn't remember the last time he had seen her there. It was either the massive Christmas debacle, or the Easter incident that no-one spoke of, that was the last straw. All those incidents had one common factor. Her partner, Cameron Parsons. 'Let's hope she hasn't brought *him*,' he said to his wife.

The homestead's dining room was the biggest room in the house, and John Blackwood sat in his work clothes at the head of the long dining table. Casey tried to remember a time he'd seen him without a work shirt and jeans on but couldn't; he guessed it may have been at his own wedding. The room was full of workers from the farm: farmhands, tractor drivers, truckies. He'd managed to rustle up a small army. Gabby sat beside him to his left and as Casey entered John pointed at the seat to his right.

Once Casey was seated, John began. 'Alright. As you all are now aware, my grandson has been missing for three days. Three days now he's been out there all alone. I won't have it. I can't think about him being out there any bloody more.' There was silence in the room and he banged his hand down on the table. 'I don't care what it takes. I want you all out there searching for him. Stop everything on the farm. The farm can wait.'

It was a huge call to make, Casey thought. They were well into final preparations for harvest. They still had weeks' worth of work and not a lot of time. 'Dad?' he asked.

John spun towards him. 'What? Don't say what I think you are about to say, Casey.' His face was getting redder as he pointed at Gabby. 'We owe this to your sister.'

Casey felt his own anger beginning to rise. 'Owe her what? We don't owe her a goddamn thing. She hasn't wanted a thing from us for years. And now all of a sudden she needs us?'

Gabby opened her mouth and John held a hand up to stop her. 'Get out,' he said in Casey's direction.

Casey stood up in a fit of rage. Who was his father to embarrass him in front of all the workers? He stormed outside onto the deck. He was the only reason the farm was still theirs. While his father played in the dirt, Casey was the one making real money.

John had shipped him off to private school when his mother had died, unable to face his own son and be the father that Casey had wanted him to be. In Sydney, Casey had thrived. It had started small, but he became a salesman of any type of drug you could think of, and had more connections than anyone back then. His grandfather had been the real businessman and he looked up to him more than anyone. In the 60s he had bought all of the neighbouring farms around Moroco during a terrible drought, and when Casey returned back to Gabinda with his new partner Tori, he was given Riverleigh, the house and farm to the east of Moroco, when he married.

Casey had a very small circle of people who knew the truth: that the giant machinery shed in the north paddock of his farm near the national highway wasn't what it looked like from the outside. It was a giant storage shed and a state-of-the-art one too. Product would flow in and out at night, interstate trucks picking up and delivering all types of drugs to the cities without ever casting too much heat on him. It was the perfect cover. Gabinda was so far away from everything that he was never bothered. It didn't hurt that the local police force seemed useless either.

But the disappearance of his nephew had thrown him. How had he gone missing at the Gabinda Show right under everyone's noses? He couldn't understand it. And when his father had told him that they had found his black hat, close to the edge of Barnes Road, he knew straightaway that he'd been taken. But to what end? He wondered if it had something to do with the family. He owed people money, and people owed him money, that was the drug business, it was always an imperfect circle. Money went one way, and never seemed to come back in a straight or straightforward line. As he stood out in the blazing sun beside his ute, he lit a cigarette while he waited for the meeting to be over. He needed to formulate a plan. He couldn't have his father organising all the workers of Moroco to go out searching. He couldn't afford the police to be doing the same thing either. If anyone realised what they had in that machinery shed, they were as good as done for.

All roads had to lead back to Cameron Parsons, he realised. His brother-in-law was a deadbeat, always had been, always would be. Casey had been using him for years to his advantage, of course. He was the only person he entrusted to sell any of the product that he had in town. *A bit of extra money never hurt anyone*, he thought. He knew that with the money he was paying him, Cameron would never fuck it up. Casey chose to pay him well over and above the market rate of what he sold. It was a compromise, he told himself. He hoped that money would end up going to his sister and nephew.

He thought back to the night of the rodeo. He had seen Matty and Cameron together near the dodgem cars in the showgrounds. Had Cameron done something terrible? He wouldn't put it past him.

That's why that night as he watched Cameron walk out the door of the pub, he realised he needed to act. He pulled his best friend Daniel aside and told him his thoughts. Daniel was the only other local in town who knew the truth of his operation. He'd always hired outside help to run the factory. He knew Daniel could be trusted, so after fabricating a story about wanting to go shoot some rabbits, to get away from their friends, he left his wife with a friend at the bar and they both climbed into Casey's Landcruiser ute, and set out to find Cameron

Parsons, and find out the truth about where Matty could have got to.

It hadn't taken long. They'd found him wandering aimlessly through a local park with his bottle of Jack in hand. Casey had pulled up and told him to get in the back. Cameron had swayed on the spot for a moment, looking like he was trying to make up his mind and then slowly climbed his way in. 'You right, Casey? Thanks for the lift, mate.'

Casey said nothing, just accelerated into the night towards the national highway. His friend Daniel stared straight ahead in the dark, looking like he was mentally preparing himself for what was going to happen next. As the wheels of the ute turned onto the wide highway, Cameron suddenly asked, 'What's goin' on? Where are you taking me?'

'Shut up,' Casey replied.

Cameron fell into an uneasy silence as Casey motored towards the back entrance of his property. He turned into the back gate where the trucks would enter and pressed the remote on his dashboard for the motorised gate. He drove through slowly and made sure it closed behind him.

'What are we doing here?' Cameron asked.

Casey and Daniel both got out and Casey nodded in his old friend's direction. Daniel pulled the black pistol out of his waistband and pointed it at Cameron through the ute window. 'Get out,' Daniel said.

Cameron opened the door slowly with both hands up. 'Casey? What the hell is going on?'

Casey lit a cigarette. 'We are going to have a talk, Cameron.'

Chapter Eighteen

Joanna met Amelia back at the Gabinda police station. In the centre of the office, Archie joined them as Amelia brought up the aerial map images on the screen of the laptop at her desk. Archie quickly brought Joanna up to speed. The SES had called off their search and had packed up the night before; there was just not enough evidence for them to continue the search, and they weren't even sure what direction they should have been heading. Also, state command had given the go ahead for Matty's name and the information about his disappearance to go public for the first time. While Joanna flew back, young Matty's face was on every channel on the evening news. Joanna knew what that meant, the media would be sure to descend very soon.

Joanna updated them on what Hattie had just found. '11:45pm last night, Matty Blackwood's phone was switched on for thirteen seconds. Just long enough for our tech to catch it. Any shorter and it wouldn't have registered.' She zoomed the map outwards, showing Gabinda north of the location.

'That's the Smith's farm. The Ford's farm skirts that boundary too,' Archie said running his hand up the line on the map.

'Ford?' Joanna asked. 'As in Neville Ford?'

'Yeah,' Archie replied.

That's interesting, Joanna thought. She looked out the window, they still had an hour or two of sunlight left. 'Alright then. I'm going to head out and check out the area.'

'I'll tag along, if that's alright,' Amelia asked.

Joanna used directions provided by Benji, who told her he would meet her at the gate of Neville's property and direct her in from there. When they arrived she found her brother alongside Dean, the first bull rider of Neville's crew she had met back on her first day in Gabinda.

'Welcome back,' Benji said with a grin. He was covered from head to toe in red dirt.

'You're a mess,' Joanna exclaimed.

Benji shrugged. 'We were practising. Last bastard nearly put me through a fence.' He made a circular motion with his left arm. 'Shoulder's bloody killing me.'

'Heard Cameron Parsons has done a runner?' Dean asked.

Amelia answered his question. 'Last seen two nights ago now, near the front of the Gabinda Hotel.'

Dean shook his head. 'Bloke's a bloody drop kick. Always has been, always will be.'

'Is there history there?' Joanna asked.

Dean spat on the ground. 'An ancient one. Cam came to Neville's farm as a young bloke. Wanted to be a bull rider. He wasn't bad at first, from what I hear.'

'And something happened?' Joanna asked.

Dean shrugged. 'All just rumours. Before my time. Neville told me once he got caught stealing. I've heard a few different versions.'

'He was selling pills to some of the riders. That's what I heard,' Benji added.

'Pills?' Joanna asked.

'Prescription stuff.' Benji laughed. 'With no prescription, of course. Oxy, Endone, Vicodin, all the hard shit.'

Joanna knew just how bad some of those pills were. After seeing what that bull had done to their friend, she understood the dangers of their profession. Pain medication like that was abused in a lot of extreme sports. Being opioids, they were as highly addictive as the more famous illicit drugs like heroin and methamphetamine. She made a mental note to circle back to that discussion with her brother. He was a bull rider, and one learning the profession could get injured quite easily. He would be one of the most susceptible if he partook in drugs like that, and she wanted to tell him how serious that type of addiction was.

Dean pointed down the dirt driveway that looked like it almost stretched to the horizon. 'Your map pointed out down this way, quicker to cut through Neville's and go over the boundary fence that way.'

'What about the Smith's?' Amelia asked.

Dean scoffed. 'Hobby farmers. They aren't here. Only come for the busy months. Post some pics on Facebook and then head back to the city.'

Joanna and Amelia climbed into the back of the farm ute and they headed down the dirt driveway. The farm was dead flat, the land barren, and Joanna spied a home in the distance on the left. 'That Neville's place?' she asked.

'Yep,' Benji replied as they passed the two-storey brick home. It had a top floor balcony overlooking the garden. 'Nev lives there with his wife Wendy. Our place is further back. That's where the training grounds are.'

They continued on and reached a fork in the dirt road. In the distance to the left was a giant shed with a variety of trailers, caravans and cars parked out the front of it. It looked like an aeroplane hangar from where Joanna was sitting. 'It's huge,' she said to no-one in particular.

Dean pointed. 'Biggest indoor practice facility in the state.' He pointed towards the eastern wall. 'Our bunkhouse is at the end of it.'

'How the hell does he afford all of this?' Amelia asked.

Dean answered. 'Pro bull riding has gone through a bit of a resurgence in Australia over the last two years. We got a new TV package that got streamed onto a couple of the big apps. Sponsors came running in. Times have been good, really good. Neville's been lucky. Nearly all the champions in the past ten years have come from his stable. He takes a percentage of their cheques as rent when they win.'

'What about the ones who don't win?' Joanna asked.

Benji laughed again. 'Like me and Dean? We work on the farm as well. It's not a bad gig. I drive tractors mostly, Dean too, but when we have spare time we are in the bull ring, training to be better riders.'

'The bull ring?'

'That's what we call it. "It's where champions are made," Neville always says.'

'Slow down. We're here,' Dean said as they pulled up in the middle of nowhere.

The group got out and Joanna referred back to her map. Hattie wasn't entirely sure but said she guessed the Apple tracking would be down to between 100 to 500 metres. It left a lot to be desired, Joanna thought. She looked out across the Smith paddock, and the knee high grass. She sighed. This was going to be like finding a needle in a haystack.

Amelia and Dean climbed over the fence and went left, forming a line and scanning the paddocks northward. Joanna and Benji turned right, heading south. She stayed about an arm-width from her brother and they both kept their eyes peeled on the land, praying for a miracle.

'What do you think about all of this?' Joanna asked him.

Benji kept his eyes peeled on the ground. 'Hard to say, really. Cameron going missing is weird to me. The guy's no good, I know that. But he's dedicated to little Matty. I've seen it.'

'How do you know Gabby Blackwood?'

Benji smiled. 'We dated a long time ago.'

Joanna spun to her brother. 'What?! Why didn't you tell me that earlier!'

Benji kept looking down. 'What was I supposed to say, Joanna? This isn't high school, fuck. We hooked up a few times when I first got to town. I met the family back then. Big show and all. But it all fell away as fast as it began. I had to go away for work, I was chasing the harvest back then so I couldn't commit. She moved on to another bloke, and then a few years later she was shacked up with Cameron. I moved on.'

'Why didn't you say anything earlier? That's why you were speaking to John Blackwood the night Matty went missing?'

Benji shrugged. 'I think he's always had a soft spot for me. He's offered me a job on more than one occasion.'

'Why didn't you take it?'

'Neville's always been kind to me. I wasn't that reliable when I was a young bloke. I bounced in and out of town a lot. Got into a lot of blues at the pub, got locked up a couple of times.'

Silence fell between the pair. Joanna didn't know whether it was the place or time, but she knew that what he had said was a potential opening. 'You know I'm sorry Benj. I'm sorry for leaving.'

Benji kicked a clod of dirt. 'Water under the bridge, sis. Don't worry about it.'

She grabbed his shoulder gently and stopped him. 'It's not. Our dad was a drunk, we both know that. He abused me and I had to get away. I was selfish back then, I didn't think that he would hurt you. I'm sorry. If I could take it all back, I would. I'll regret leaving every single day for the rest of my life.' She wrapped him up in a hug. 'I love you and I don't want to lose you.'

Benji pulled back. 'You're not gonna lose me. I forgive you.' He chuckled. 'Shit, I would've done the same thing if I had the chance.' He looked back down at the ground and turned away. 'Besides, he'd slowed down a lot by then. He wasn't the man he was when you were around, I could usually fight him off.'

'Joanna!'

They spun around to see Amelia in the distance waving in their direction. Dean was against the fence line and the three ran over to her. There, in between the knee-high blades of dried glass was an iPhone in a blue case. 'That what you're looking for?' Benji asked.

Joanna bent down with a clear plastic evidence bag and picked it up. 'Yep. Hopefully we can get some information out of it. Better yet, some prints or DNA.'

Chapter Nineteen

Joanna's initial excitement at the news of finding Matty's phone dwindled over the next few days. The phone had been factory reset sometime before it was last turned on and when Hattie discovered it. DNA and prints were found on the phone, but there were no matches in the police database.

She returned to Gabby's home the day after with Amelia to interview her again. The news of the phone retrieval had made the 6pm news and Joanna could tell by the mother's nervous energy that she assumed that they were getting close. In truth, Joanna felt as far away from finding Matty as the first night he went missing.

Hattie's data scrape had provided no further evidence and the vendors from the show continued to slowly drip feed CCTV footage that they thought was worthwhile. Constable Webb had the smart idea of checking the local petrol stations cameras and any other cameras in the main street on the night of disappearance, but came up empty-handed from that too. As she sat in the office reading interview notes from her first interview with Gabby, something inside her seemed to deflate. She realised that she might not have an answer for this case. That young Matty might be gone forever.

***

John Blackwood sat in his office and looked at his phone. It was late and he watched on the gate cameras as Casey's Landcruiser ute came through the opening and headed towards the storage shed. Casey had texted him idea, and although he didn't want to upset his daughter, he had a terrible feeling that Cameron was involved in his grandson's disappearance somehow; he just wasn't sure how.

He got into his ute and took the back road that connected his son's farm with his. Casey had come home to him as a different kid than when he had gone away to school. The softness of his teenage personality had gone. The cut and thrust of private school life in the city had given him a surprisingly hard edge that he never pictured his son having. Casey was the spitting image of his mother, and his late wife, Jeanette. Sometimes he wondered whether he was so hard on him because of it, whether he resented the fact that she was gone and that his son was here in her place. It had been ten years now since she'd passed away from breast cancer, and he wondered sometimes what his life would look like if she were still around.

Casey had laid it all out on the table for him back then. There was no stutter in his voice, just firm and assertive statements. He spoke in facts and figures. He said he had got involved with a crowd that dealt drugs. He had started dealing himself. He had got good at it, really good. John remembered the night well, he felt like his son was challenging him: was he going to be with him or against him? John listened to the story and realised he felt alive again for the first time in a long time. He had nothing to lose and everything to gain. If it all turned to shit, he was going to be giving it all to Casey anyway, Gabby was out of the picture. They spent the next year planning methodically; Casey was past the seller stage and wanted to move into the big time. He had a plan and it was a good one: he explained to his contacts in the city the location of his family's farms, and how the national highways ran straight past. You could go north, south, east or west from here and it was the perfect location for a storage point. They had jumped at the chance.

That night though, the shed was quiet. Casey had turned away shipments for the next week while the heat was still in town, and it was costing them a lot of money. John pulled through the gate and parked next to his son's ute. A single light near the office was on and he got out and walked inside.

Cameron Parsons sat slumped in a chair near the door. Casey stood near the entrance and turned as John walked in. John could see Cameron's face, he was bleeding from the mouth and a black eye was beginning to appear.

'Anything?' John asked.

Casey shook his head. 'Nothing. I don't know, Dad. He seems pretty adamant.'

He walked on past his son and Cameron began to plead. 'John, please, help me. I got nothin' to do with any of this, I swear.'

John knelt down on one knee. Cameron's left eye had begun to close, and he could see one of his front teeth was chipped. 'Can you see where you are, Cameron?'

Cameron looked around. The shed was nondescript, and to the untrained eye could pass for another farm storage shed, but he was smart enough, he knew what being brought here meant. He nodded slowly. 'Yeah.'

'This is it. This is the operation. I've brought you here because I trust you. You've seen it now. You got my balls in a vice. You can see now that you've got the power, right?'

John's speech had got the desired response. Even though Cameron was tied up in the chair, his posture straightened, his chin lifted, his eyes were clearer. John needed him to think he had a level of control. 'I'm telling you, I don't know anything. I swear. He was sitting beside me and told me he was going for ice cream. Then he was gone. I don't know where he is.'

'You still selling?' John asked.

Cameron's shoulders lifted in a half shrug. 'Time to time. What's that got to do with it? When money gets tight.'

'Who to?'

'No-one in particular. Sold a bit at the show, sell a bit in the towns over. Don't want anyone to recognise me.'

'What about Neville's guys?'

'Sure. Sell a bit to them, mostly the pain pills. None of the real hard shit.'

John watched him speak and realised how much of a liability his son-in-law had become. He was a loose cannon, he could mouth off at any time, and put the whole operation in jeopardy. He needed him to realise that he was dispensable. John pulled out the pistol he had in the back of his waistband, a stubby nosed, black and menacing looking thing, and pointed it into Cameron's gut. 'I want you off the piss for the next month. I want you out asking around all the last people you sold to. Ask them about your son and if they know anything about his disappearance.'

Tears rolled down Cameron's bloody face. 'I want to find him.'

'You need to find him,' John replied.

He stood up and headed back to Casey. 'Outside,' he said.

Casey followed him into the dark. 'What do you think?' Casey asked.

'Just keep him here for a few days. Let him sweat it a little more,' John replied. 'He knows he can't say anything to anyone if we let him go. We'll bloody kill him if he does.'

'Alright then.'

John lit a cigarette and looked up at the stars. 'He has to be involved in all of this somehow.'

Chapter Twenty

He couldn't go on much longer. He realised when he saw it on the news that he'd made a terrible decision. He didn't know how to get the word out without it coming back to him. He wondered what to do, how to get rid of the problem before the heat came on. The police were searching nearby. John Blackwood and his band of thugs were searching. Soon they would get him if he didn't take action. He needed the problem to go away, and go away for good.

***

Joanna lasted another week at Gabinda and her daily calls with the Chief Inspector ended up with her relaying the same information over and over. She had Matty's hat, his phone, the child at the show's eyewitness sighting of the man in the black hat. It wasn't a lot, but it was something. Whatever momentum she had in those first few days was long gone and the Chief ended up making the decision for her: she was required back in Sydney. Nick's recovery was going better than expected and he was due back on the job in the next few weeks. She had been texting him on and off and could tell he was itching to get back. She was to come back and prepare for his return and a new case load.

For her last night in town she took Amelia, Benji and Glenn out for dinner at the pub. It was a subdued affair, with the whole group being sad at her departure. Joanna secretly thought Amelia might be enjoying having a competent cop at her side for once, with the Inspector ready to retire and the other constables all still green. Amelia told her as much, and said she wished she could stay on for longer, and that it would only take one break and they would find him, she had insisted.

After their conversation during the search for the phone, Joanna felt like her relationship with Benji had strengthened. She felt a connection with him that she hadn't felt in a long time, and promised him that she would do her best to return to Gabinda again, or try and catch him riding at a show when the rodeo season started again. She told him Nick would love to meet him. She knew the two men would get along well.

Glenn sat quietly and listened to the group as they spoke. Joanna had been sharing a few texts with him when she had a spare moment and she liked the guy. She could tell he was disappointed that she was leaving but he had been a gentleman about it. He told her to not be a stranger, and if she was ever back in the area to give her a call. It was refreshing for her to meet someone so respectful, and they had shared a kiss outside the pub when Benji and Amelia left. He wanted to go back to her motel, but she told him she wasn't ready. In truth, she still felt self-conscious about the burn scars on her legs and didn't feel like having the conversation about it with someone she might never see again.

***

Nick stood at the entrance of the police headquarters and stared upwards at the hulking glass building. The past few weeks had been a whirlwind and he wasn't sure what this visit would bring. The Chief had told him that his door was always open, and that whenever he was ready, he should come back and chat with him about the future. His recovery had been going better than expected. His therapist had told him he was one of the best patients she had ever had. He was fit, still strong for his age and showed a determination she had only seen demonstrated by the athletes she worked with. He worked hard to regain his strength and, although he knew he had a long way to go, he was certain he could handle the day-to-day operations of being a homicide detective again.

Joanna walked out of the glass doors to greet him, with a smile on her face. She was dressed in navy-blue pants and a crisp, white dress shirt. Her make-up was immaculate and her hair was styled in a way he'd never seen before. 'Morning,' he said, matching her smile. 'You're looking very professional.'

Joanna blushed as she held her arms up. 'Do I look stupid? God, I feel stupid. Everyone in here is so well dressed. I thought I'd better up my game a bit.'

'Dress for the job you want, not the job you have,' Nick replied with a wink. 'You'll have the Chief Inspector's job in no time.'

'I'm not sure I want that job, she said with a laugh as she turned towards the doors. 'How are you feeling? Are you okay?'

'Better than ever. Ready to go.'

'Alright then. C'mon, the Chief's waiting for us.'

Nick watched everyone closely as they walked in through the main entrance of the police building, and scanned themselves in through the metal detectors. It started at the reception; he watched as the two young women, one he recognised, whispering something to each other and pointing. Joanna headed to the bank of elevators and pressed the button for the sixth floor. She referred to the two women. 'You're the talk of the place today. Everyone knows you're back.'

Nick said nothing. He didn't know what to say or how to feel just yet. He had a feeling that whatever the Chief was going to say to him would be bad news. A growing feeling had grown in the pit of his stomach as the weeks progressed, he felt like the Chief was considered benching him forever. He wasn't going to spend his future at a desk. It was on the road or nothing, and he was prepared to hand in his badge if it came to it.

The general buzz of office conversation fell quiet as Nick stepped onto the floor. There was more pointing and whispering in his direction. Nods of approval then returning to their tasks. *The oddity had been observed and all was normal*, he thought to himself.

Superintendent Timmins, the leader of the state drug squad and good friend of the Chief Inspector, walked out of his office and straight up to him. He was a tough cookie, and it was rare to see a smile on his face, but Nick's return had done just that. He patted him on the back. 'Welcome home, mate. Bloody great work, you two,' he said to them both.

They continued onwards as Joanna whispered under her breath, 'I don't think he knows my name.'

Nick tried to keep a straight face as they reached the Chief's office. It was exactly the same as the last time he'd been there, from what he could remember, and he looked over his desk to the floor-to-ceiling windows and the Sydney Harbour in the distance.

'Nick, welcome back, mate,' the Chief said with a grin. He reached over the table and shook Nick's hand, he was always much more formal in the office. 'How are you feeling?'

'Good. Rehab has gone better than I thought. Back to fighting shape.'

The Chief's eyes seemed to scan over his body for a second and then rested back on his face. If he was looking for some kind of weakness, or any kind of difference, he didn't seem to notice any. 'Good man. I'm glad. I thought we'd lost you back there.'

'I told him he's down to eight lives,' Joanna said.

The Chief laughed. 'Maybe even seven. Alright, take a seat.' The Chief placed both hands down on the table. 'Okay, I'm not going to beat around the bush here. As I said back in Blarnie, I've got some pressure from up above about getting you here on a desk, Nick.' Nick opened his mouth to speak but the Chief lifted his hand. 'Let me finish. But I know the Commissioner well. And he knows you well, and he has read the reports on the way you and Joanna operate. Now, I've had requests from multiple departments to pick up Joanna if you were to stay based here. But ultimately, I told the Commissioner you'll make the final call.'

Nick looked across at his partner. She had runs on the board now and she was wanted. He felt like he'd only just started teaching her what it was to be a good detective. A smile slowly formed on her lips in his direction. He could read her mind.

'I want to keep being a detective if that's okay, Chief. I know there are still good things we can do out there.'

The folder on the Chief's desk snapped shut and he placed it back in his drawer. 'Alright then. That settles it. Welcome back, Detective.'

Jason Summers

Chapter Twenty-One

He raced along the dirt track as fast as his bike would take him. Now daylight savings had started he had more time to get down there and try and catch as many yabbies as possible but he knew he had to be wary: while the Smith family didn't live on the property, they were still likely to turn up any day now, as school holidays started in Victoria at a different time to his so he knew he had to watch out.

The dirt track that ran the length of their farm was rough and unmaintained. He crashed over the bumps with ease on the new mountain bike his mum had got him for his birthday. It was heaps better than his BMX.

He'd asked his friend Harry if he wanted to come down with him, but Harry was grounded for fighting with his brother. He wasn't too bothered. It was a nice night and the yabbies had been biting like crazy the week before, it just meant all the more for him. Tied on the back of his bike was an esky for his catch and three opera nets. His dad had told him these nets weren't allowed anymore but this was Gabinda, who was going to stop him?

The dam was bigger than most farm dams in the area and with the shade of the gum trees spread around it meant that it had become a popular swimming hole for the kids in the town. They all knew about the Smith family and the fact that they didn't live there most of the year. They all knew not to go there as soon as the Smiths returned, but word around school had been quiet and the weather was cool, so he knew he'd be fine to try and catch some yabbies in peace. He pulled up at the dam, rested his bike up against a tree and got busy setting the rotten meat in the opera nets. He then slowly dispersed them along the edge of the dam, trying to get as close to the logs as possible because his dad told him that's where yabbies were most likely to go.

He walked back up the bank near his bike and pulled out his phone. He texted his mum to tell her what he was up to and was just about to take a photo on his Snapchat when he noticed something poking out of the water. He stood up to get a better look. There was a blue shape in the water, and from where he was standing it looked like a dummy, kind of like the ones in the clothes shops his mum took him to.

He walked down the bank slowly and over towards a felled gum tree that ran out closer to the odd shape. He took his runners off and grabbed a long stick from the bank. He had another thought, sometimes livestock drowned in dams; he wondered if it was a dead sheep. But then he remembered the Smith family had no sheep or cattle from what he could remember. He checked the log was sturdy, then slowly and surely walked down the thick trunk closer towards the shape. It was still just a blue bulge, bobbing up and down as his weight pushed the log down, which caused a ripple effect on the water.

His stick was long and he made sure to keep a safe distance. He reached out with it and landed the point of it perfectly on top of the shape. He slowly pulled it towards him, and ever so gently the shape rolled in his direction.

When he realised what he was looking at he jumped back in terror and screamed, almost flipping off the log.

***

Joanna drove along the open country highway as Nick did his best to find the next local radio station. It was a gift of his she had discovered soon after she started working with him; he seemed to have every major station in each region of the state pre-saved in his memory from past visits, and they were never without bearable music. She felt at ease being back in his presence, and that comfort seemed reciprocated by him. They spoke in fits and spurts as the thoughts came to them, but she never felt uncomfortable in the silence with him like she would with someone else.

They were heading towards Dubbo to meet with a local sergeant to discuss a two-year-old cold case. She had asked the Chief about heading back to Gabinda, but he told her unless there were any breaks in the case there was no point wasting their time, the missing person side of it could be dealt with by the local team. She knew the Chief wasn't going to put them on anything big to start off with and she wondered whether Nick had asked him privately for a few weeks to work his way back up to match fitness. After her time in Gabinda, she was happy to slow down a little bit.

As she drove, she thought about Gabby Blackwood and the worry she must be going through. Although she technically wasn't on the case anymore, she had spoken to Amelia over FaceTime to get up to speed while she was packing the night before. Cameron Parsons hadn't resurfaced and the Inspector had the local team doubling down and looking further into him and into his past, as he seemed sure he had something to do with it all. Joanna wasn't so sure, and Amelia wasn't either. She thought back to the night in the arena and Cameron sitting in the stands with Gabby. She still wondered about the cowboy in the black hat, and what connection he had to it all.

They arrived in Dubbo and their interview with the local sergeant was fruitful. Word on the street in town was that a prominent local drug dealer had been mouthing off about how he had been involved in the murder of local man Jesse Perkins the year earlier. It had been grizzly, Joanna thought as she had scrolled through the images of the crime scene photos. Fingernails had been removed, his left knee had been busted. Nick said that he must have owed some serious money and she wholeheartedly agreed. When they were done with the sergeant, they headed out to find a quiet place to map out their next move. As they walked back out of the Dubbo police station, Joanna checked her phone. She had two missed calls from Amelia and three more from the Chief Inspector. She showed the phone screen to Nick and he gave her a look of curiosity. 'What's that all about?'

As she went to dial the Chief, Benji was calling her. Something big must have happened, she realised, and as she answered her brain was already putting two and two together: they must have found Matty.

'Benji,' she answered. 'What's wrong? Please tell me this is good news.'

Benji's voice was flat and expressionless. 'Hey sis. Not good news. They found Matty Blackwood. He's dead.'

Joanna stopped on the spot. Her mind was racing with millions of questions. Nick sensed her change in body language and he stopped as well. 'Where?' she asked.

'The Smith's farm. In their dam.'

'The Smith's farm. Isn't that where we found the phone?'

'About a kilometre away from there,' he replied. 'Near their house.'

'Jesus,' she replied. 'We were so close.' Her phone beeped, she could see the Chief was calling again. 'I'll call you back, my boss is calling.'

Joanna ended the call and placed the Chief on loudspeaker. 'Chief, sorry I missed your call. Nick's here with me.'

'Have you heard the news?'

Joanna nodded. 'My brother just called me.'

'They find the kid?' Nick asked, unsure of what had been said.

'Unfortunately, they did. Young kid was fishing in a dam out the outskirts of town. He found Matty Blackwood's body in the water, deceased,' The Chief replied.

'Shit,' Nick replied. 'That poor kid.'

The Chief was silent for a moment and then continued, 'This changes things for us, of course. Joanna, I think you need to head back to Gabinda. I'm getting pressure for answers from up above The case is all over the news still and once this gets out things are going to go crazy.'

Joanna smiled. She was ready. Everything was still fresh in her mind so she wanted to get back there as soon as possible. She looked across at her partner. It had only been a few days back on the job and he still wasn't quite the same, but she knew he was ready for a challenge. 'We'll head there straightaway.'

'Nick. You up for this? Let me know if you still need more time. I can get Detective Sergeant Romac out to assist.'

Joanna watched him closely. His face was set and his expression was one of determination. 'I'm ready.'

'Alright, I'll let the Inspector know you're on your way.'

Joanna hung up the phone. 'You sure you're ready?'

'Yep. Let's go and catch these bastards.'

Chapter Twenty-Two

Gabby had finally succumbed to her dad's wishes. With Cameron missing and Matty still nowhere to be found, he wanted her back at Moroco in their family home until the police figured out where both Matty and Cameron had gone.

She sat on the back deck as the sun set over the beautiful horizon. The wheat crops that had been planted had taken well and grown perfectly her dad had said, and she watched the crops swaying gently in a light breeze in the distance. She smoked a cigarette slowly. She had given up smoking a few years earlier, but the first morning she had woken up after Matty disappeared she had raided Cameron's drawer in their bedroom and found a pack, she needed them for the stress. She sipped from a wine glass and felt the bitter-sweet liquid beginning to make her feel lightheaded at the mixture of cigarettes and alcohol.

Her childhood home hadn't changed in the eight years it had been since she was there on her last ever visit. It had been a different time, she had been young and stupid back then, she realised now. She had hated her father for a long time after her mother's death, and she wished she could take back some of the things that she had said. She still didn't know why she had resented him so much. After their final blow up he had given her space and hadn't pushed her to try and bring her back into the fold. Casey had tried a few times, told her to bury the hatchet, but she wasn't going to listen to her little brother; she wanted an apology directly from her dad.

Matty's disappearance had brought them back together, and she felt so grateful to watch him and her brother searching relentlessly for her son. Cameron going missing wasn't as simple. He was a damaged soul, and although they had been together now for a long time, she felt like there were parts of him she would never understand. The police had dropped hints at their ideas that he may have been involved in Matty's disappearance, but she wasn't having any of that talk. She pictured him holed up in some motel room far away, drunk or high, ruminating on the decisions he made the night of the rodeo and blaming himself for Matty going missing. He would turn up. She knew it.

Dust in the distance was her first inkling of visitors and her curiosity piqued when she saw that it was a four-wheel drive police car. She checked her phone and saw no missed calls and wondered if they were about to deliver good news. 'Dad! The police!'

John Blackwood popped his head out from the kitchen. 'Have you heard from them today? Wonder what this is about?'

'Maybe they've found Matty,' she said, full of hope.

The car pulled up beside her and Archie, the Inspector, and Amelia got out. She ran down the steps of the deck two at a time, praying for a miracle. She was halfway across the grass in the front yard when she saw the solemn expressions on their faces, and their hats tucked formally under their arms.

'NO!!' she screamed as she reached them. 'No, no, no, no!'

She fell to her knees at Amelia's feet as the tears exploded out of her eyes. All the air in her body felt like it had come out. Amelia knelt down to her eye level. 'C'mon Gabby, hop up.' She grabbed her hand and pulled her slowly up. By that time John had reached them and could see his daughter's reaction.

'What happened? What is it?'

The Inspector delivered the news. 'Matty was found earlier today. I'm sorry to tell you he is deceased.'

Gabby's cries reached a crescendo and a flock of birds flew out of the nearby towering gum trees in protest. John held his daughters hand as his rage began to build. 'Where? Who is the bastard that killed my grandson?'

The Inspector looked at Amelia. 'We just don't have that kind of information right now, John.'

'Bullshit you don't!' John bellowed.

'We have two of the best homicide detectives in the state on their way. They'll be here in the next few hours to assess the scene. As soon as they are satisfied, his body will be released to you.'

'I need to make some calls,' John said as he turned and walked away. He stopped near the bottom of the deck and turned back. 'You lot better find the bastards that did this! Because if I find 'em first I'm going to kill 'em!'

Amelia gave Gabby as much of the scant details she was allowed to give and then the two cops left. Gabby stood rooted on the spot unable to move. Matty. Her little boy. Gone forever. She didn't want to live any more.

***

It was dark by the time Nick and Joanna reached Gabinda. Joanna had left her phone on speaker while the local sergeant updated them on what they'd found so far. Nick drove and listened intently. Having another case that needed answers made him feel rejuvenated. He couldn't explain it, but he felt whole again as they entered town and parked out front of the local police station.

Joanna made the introductions. There was Archie, the elderly Inspector who now looked like he wished he had retired a few years earlier. There was a Constable Thomas Webb, who looked like he had stepped out of the academy a week ago, and finally Sergeant Amelia Rossi. Nick watched her speak and realised that she was the heartbeat of the station. Everyone listened to every word closely and he made a mental note to pull her aside and ask her about Joanna's performance in Gabinda when she was first here, and also ask her what her own thoughts on the case were.

The Chief had called and advised they were flying in two crime scene technicians from Sydney. Their flight was due to land in the next few hours at Gabinda airport, which really was a single aeroplane hangar for a crop-dusting company with a grass runway. Nick and Joanna were to pick them up and sort accommodation for the night for them.

There was a small amount of crime scene photos spread across the table. Nick looked at them closely. The body had been pulled out of the dam and gently placed on the edge of the bank. The Inspector had advised he had two other constables at the scene over night to keep an eye on everything and then told them about their visit to Moroco a few hours earlier, and John Blackwood's reaction to the news.

'Pretty understandable,' Nick replied. 'He's the big man in town. He had his whole life planned out for him. Now he's planning lives for others. This wasn't on the cards for him or his family, I get it. He has no control, it's up to us now and he's probably spiralling.'

'I told Nick about that first night when he tried to give me money,' she added to the group.

'All just a power play,' Nick said. 'We've seen plenty like him before.' He pointed down at the map. 'Tell me more about the location.'

'The Smith farm is nestled between Neville Ford's property and the Kessler farm. The Smith's are out of towners, from Melbourne. They come up from time to time, masquerading as people from the bush,' Amelia said. 'It's a hobby farm. They drive Range Rovers and their clothing is immaculate.'

Nick pointed down at the satellite image. 'Looks like a small bit of wheat or barley here? They must do a little bit of work out there?'

Amelia shrugged. 'I think the Kessler's give them a hand with that mostly.'

Nick pointed at the satellite image at the location of Neville Ford's indoor rodeo arena. 'And this building is Neville Ford's?'

Amelia nodded. 'Biggest indoor bull riding training facility in the southern hemisphere.'

Nick eyed Neville's house, the bunkhouse and then the arena. He looked at the cars, utes, caravans and trailers all spread around the area. The dam from that location was around two kilometres as the crow flies. He then looked at the Kessler farm. There was a house, a machinery shed and tractors, trucks and a header lined up in a line beside it. Preparing for harvest, he assumed, it was that time of the year. He looked at his watch. 'Joanna, we've got crime scene services landing in an hour. We'll need to go shortly.'

Amelia seemed to be watching him closely. 'What are you thinking?' she asked him.

Nick looked at his partner. 'Joanna's the one you should be asking,' he replied. 'I need to look around at the scene and talk to some people before I can come to any conclusions.'

Chapter Twenty-Three

Casey stood in the kitchen of his home at Riverleigh and watched the sun set. His dad had called him and told him the news. Matty was dead. Someone had found his body earlier in the day, he didn't know where or how. Casey realised straightaway they had a big problem: if Matty's body had just been found, how could Cameron be involved? Cameron was still being kept in the office of the storage shed and had been there for two weeks now. Casey had beaten him three times now, to the point he'd make himself feel queasy, but Cameron was stronger than he had ever thought he would be. He had sworn on his life that he hadn't been involved in Matty's disappearance and Casey now realised he hadn't been lying.

'Are you okay?' his wife Tori asked.

He turned around from the sink. 'Yeah. I guess.'

She shook her head. 'Poor Gabby. I just can't imagine. Is she still at Moroco?'

'Yeah.'

'What are you going to do Casey?' He knew what she was referring to.

'I'm going to let him go. Gabby's going to need him around I guess, more than ever.'

'What if he says something?'

Casey had thought of that too, he had voiced his concerns to his father, but he was a more trusting man than Casey was. 'I think Dad's going to pay him off.'

Tori sipped from her glass of wine. 'It's his call. He's taking a big risk.'

'I know.'

Casey sped down the back road towards the machinery shed and pressed the button for the electronic gate. He pulled through the opening and parked at the door of the shed in the darkness and cautiously got out of the ute. He had to tell Cameron, he knew that, and he braced himself for the man's reaction. The bloke had taken an absolute beating and then some, and now here Casey was to deliver the worst news anyone could hear: their child was dead.

He opened the door and peered into the darkness. 'Hello?'

'In here,' Cameron replied.

He walked out through the door into the office. Casey had ended up opening the small office up for Cameron and he had been sleeping on the couch. There was a toilet and a small kitchenette and Casey had dropped off small amounts of food to him, even though his father had told him not to.

Cameron was sitting on the couch, his face was blackened and bruised. He seemed to lower himself down onto the couch in worry of another beating. 'What now? I'll tell ya once Casey, I'll tell ya a thousand times, I don't bloody know what happened to him! I don't know where he's gone.'

Casey stood in the doorway and realised he wasn't sure how to break the news to his brother-in-law. His face was a mess, with one eye closed over from where he'd hit him with the butt of his pistol and his lip was split from where he'd punched him. He stunk, the office didn't have a shower and suddenly Casey felt pity for him and a disdain for the way he had acted.

He didn't know how to say it, so he just blurted it out, 'Matty's dead, Cameron. They found his body today.'

Cameron flew up from the couch as his mouth opened slowly. He dropped to his knees and placed his head into his hands and started to sob, a loud guttural cry came from him. 'No!!! No, he's fuckin' not!' He looked back up into Casey's eyes. 'Tell me you're joking?'

'We don't have much more information than that, but the coppers came this afternoon and told Gabby.'

Cameron let out a sob at the sound of his partner's name. 'Gab.' He stood back up, his face full of determination. 'You gotta let me see her, Casey.'

Casey stepped aside in the doorway. 'You're free to go.'

The words seemed to trigger something in Cameron and Casey watched as his face turned an ugly shade of red. 'Free to go? You had me fuckin locked up here for weeks while my boy was out there! I told you all I had nothin' to fuckin' to do with it!'

Casey took it all on straight, he knew he deserved the vitriol and hate Cameron was throwing his way. 'I don't know what you want me to say, Cameron. Dad ordered this. I'm sorry, alright? We made the wrong call.'

Cameron went to walk past Casey. 'The wrong fuckin' call,' he mumbled. 'Wait til Gabby hears about thi—'

Casey held his hand out on Cameron's chest stopping him from exiting the office. 'Gabby won't be finding out a thing. You're not going to tell her a word. You're going to tell her you went a few towns over and got in a bar fight, that you've been holed up in some shithole motel while you recover.'

'Why would I do that?' Cameron asked.

Casey pointed back behind him onwards into the shed. 'Do you want to be a part of this? As in a real part of this?'

Cameron turned and looked at the stacks and stacks of pallets. 'Yeah. I do.'

Casey smiled. 'I spoke to Dad. He's going to give you some cash. Set you and Gabby back up a bit better alright? We'll get you involved out here, make you a part of all this. You've just got to promise that you don't say a word about what happened here.'

'Alright. You got my word.'

'Good,' Casey replied. 'Because if you don't do what we say, you're fuckin' dead.'

***

Gabby lay on the leather lounge suite in the living area of the farmhouse. A movie played quietly in the background and she watched the screen vacantly, her mind unable to decipher the images in front of her. Her son was dead. Matty. Her little boy.

Her miracle. She felt the loss and emptiness like a weight pushing down on her so hard she felt like she was being crushed. She couldn't imagine a life without him.

She knew by now that the news would be all over town. Her phone had soon exploded with messages and calls from her friends and loved ones. She had put it upstairs in the drawer in her childhood bedroom. She was incapable of answering, she couldn't even think of what words she would say.

The headlights of an incoming car bounced off the wall above the television and she ignored it. She hoped it wasn't anyone who needed to see her, she wasn't ready to face anyone just yet. John walked out from his office and looked at her and then continued to the front door as the car pulled up. 'Jesus Christ.'

She looked at the expression on his face. 'What? What is it?'

'It's Cameron,' John replied with a smile.

Gabby stood up from the couch and ran to the door. Casey's Landcruiser ute sat in the driveway and he stood on the front lawn looking at the house. She pushed past her dad and cried out as she ran into Cameron's arms, 'Cameron!'

Cameron met her in the centre of the yard and wrapped her into a tight embrace as she felt herself fall into him. She couldn't believe he was okay. She needed him now more than ever and they both stood on the lawn and cried until they were out of tears. Casey headed up into the house with her father and it wasn't until she pulled back to get a better look at Cameron that she realised what she was seeing. He looked like he had taken the beating of his life. The left side of his face was yellow with bruising and his eye was half closed with a purple tinge to his eyelid. His mouth was cut and there was a deep cut close to his eye as well, and when he tried to smile it was lopsided. He looked deformed.

'What the hell happened to you?' she asked.

He held both of her hands tightly. 'I fucked up, babe. I couldn't face ya'. I was watchin' Matty when he went missing and now he's gone.'

Gabby looked at her partner. 'Cameron. Where have you been?'

He shrugged. 'Ended up near Cobar. Stayed at an old mate's joint. Got into a fight my third night there at the pub.' He stopped for a moment. 'My fault really. I think I was looking for a beating.'

'It's been weeks though, Cam?' Gabby replied.

He let go of her hands. 'I know. I got a motel room and tried to recover. I drank and smoked. I didn't know what else to do. I never wanted to come back. I don't want to be the reason he got taken. I didn't have anything to do with it. And now he's gone,' he cried.

Gabby wrapped her arms around him again. She tried to imagine what his mind had been going through over the past few weeks, the guilt and the shame, she didn't wish it on anyone. 'It's not your fault. I know you didn't have anything to do with it.'

Jason Summers

Chapter Twenty-Four

Nick stood at the edge of the dam and bent down on one knee to feel the water. The morning sun was already beating down and he could feel it burning the back of his neck. The water was already warming up. He looked back at the trees and the thick branch of the gum tree that protruded over the water. He could see the remnants of a rope swing tied around it, level with the edge of the water. It made sense because the local sergeant had said it was a popular swimming hole for the local kids, and he could see why.

Matty Blackwood's body lay across the bank on his back merely metres from the edge of the water. There was a shade tent put up over it by the crime scene technicians he'd picked up the night before, and he watched as Joanna spoke with them and pointed to something on Matty's body.

He knew one of the crime scene techs, a man around his age who had worked a few homicides in the city with him when he was still based there. His name was Troy and Nick knew he had a reputation for being one of the best. His partner, a younger woman named Lucy, he didn't know.

He slipped under blue and white crime scene tape that the local sergeant had put up. She stood off to the side along with the young constable, clearly intimidated by the whole thing.

'Have a look at this, Nick,' Joanna said, pointing down at Matty's shoes.

Nick knelt down and looked closely. He wore runners. They were a faded blue and red after their time in the water. He looked closer into the grooves of the soles. 'What is it?'

Troy held an evidence bag in his hand. 'I've scraped it for samples. We'll get it tested and get it back to you.'

Nick walked over to the table and grabbed some gloves and one of the picking tools. He knelt back down and scraped a small amount of the brown matter out between the ridges in the sole and looked closer at it. Then he smelled it. 'It's cow shit,' he looked up at the younger tech's scrunched up face. 'Sorry, manure.'

Joanna looked around the wide area. 'Cow manure? No cows here.'

'No,' Nick replied. 'Smith family is grain. Same with the Kessler's.'

'Closest place who has cows would be the Ford property,' Joanna replied, reading his mind.

'We'll need to go have a chat with them,' Nick said. 'No socks either. That's odd. What else have you got?'

Troy held an iPad in his hands. 'Damage to the neck and windpipe. Blood clotting in the eyes. I can't say for certain until the autopsy, but I'd guess he was strangled to death.'

'Not drowned?' Nick asked.

'Hard to say, like I said. But all indications are strangulation right now.'

'He was held somewhere,' Joanna added, pointing at his little body. 'He's still in the same clothes as the night he went missing.' Nick watched her closely as her eyes shone with tears. 'Six weeks. That poor little bugger would've been so scared.'

Nick placed a hand on her shoulder. 'You okay? You don't need to be here if this is too hard.'

Joanna shook her head. 'No. I'm good.'

'Any DNA you think you'll be able to pick up?' Nick asked.

'There's some skin underneath one of his fingernails that I don't think is his. I'm going to get samples of that and get it tested.'

'Good work,' Nick replied.

'Local coroner is an hour away. He's going to come and pick up our vic. We are going to head straight to Dubbo to work from there. Soon as we find out any more, we'll let you know,' Troy said.

Nick and Joanna walked away from under the shade as the techs continued to work. He stopped just out of earshot of the local sergeant and constable. The fresh air and sunshine were making him feel better and better by the minute. He had a mystery and wanted answers more than anything. 'What do you think?' he asked Joanna.

'I just don't get it,' she replied. 'If he'd been held all that time, why? To what aim?'

'Money is the first guess,' Nick said. 'The Blackwood's are the richest family in the region, you all say.'

'But no-one ever reached out as far as we know.'

Nick scratched his chin. 'We need to talk to Gabby Blackwood.'

He walked further up the rise to the local sergeant and constable. 'You guys alright?'

They both nodded. The young constable looked green in the gills. Your first dead body was always a real experience. Nick thought back to his. He could still picture it clear as day. 'Sergeant. What can you tell me about Gabby Blackwood that we don't know already?'

Amelia pulled her glasses off and placed them on her head. 'It's hard to say. She's a law-abiding citizen. I've never had to deal with her much. She'd been pointed out to me a few times in passing. There was always a lot of town gossip around why she was disowned by John Blackwood.'

'Disowned?' Nick asked. 'That's interesting.'

'I think it's honestly just because of her partner Cameron. John never liked him, from what I've heard. I don't know whether there was much more to it.'

'Where does she work?' Nick asked.

'The doctor's office. She's a receptionist there.'

'A receptionist?' Joanna asked as she thought back. 'The night of the rodeo. When Bryce the bull rider was seriously injured. When I met her, she told me she was a nurse? That's why I called her down. To ask if she could help.'

'I've never seen her do anything in that capacity,' Amelia said.

'That's strange,' Nick said. Why would she lie? He pointed to the east, towards the Ford property. 'What about Neville Ford?' he asked.

'What about him?'

'Any trouble from his property at all over the years?'

Amelia shrugged. 'Not from him, no. His riders would get in the odd bar fight. Two a few years back got into a major blue over a ute. Apparently challenged each other to a "ride off." Winner took the ute. When the bloke who owned the ute realised he'd lost, it was on for young and old.'

Nick said nothing in reply, he just turned and walked away towards the farm. He could see the rooftop of the two-storey farmhouse in the distance along with the hulking outline of the training sheds. Joanna joined him. 'What are you thinking?'

He smiled and looked at her. 'C'mon. Thought you'd be able to read my mind by now.'

'I'll have a go. First we need to check out the Smith's place. See if they're home. If not, at least contact them to let them know what's happened out here. Then, I think we head to the Blackwood's. Speak with Gabby, she's holed up there from what

Amelia's saying. Try and speak with John Blackwood if he's around as well.'

'Good start,' Nick said. She was a fast learner.

'And then we go to the Ford's. Speak with Neville. See if he knows anything. Maybe try the bunkhouse? I can speak with Benji and get him to rustle up as many of the guys there for a chat as we can. He'd be happy to help. Plus, he's dying to meet you.'

Chapter Twenty-Five

John Blackwood had retreated to his study again. He had watched his daughter's elation at finding her partner alive and felt good in his heart about letting him go. Twenty grand it had cost him to pay for Cameron's silence. *It was nothing really*, he thought. For Gabby to have him and have some sort of happiness was something, even though it didn't bring little Matty back.

He poured himself a generous glass of whiskey and leaned back in his sagging old office chair. His laptop was shut, his phone was in the kitchen. He was alone with his thoughts. He looked at the gold-framed photograph of his wife Jeanette, which sat proudly on one side of his desk. He wondered if he would have told her the truth, whether he would have confided in her. He doubted it. The whiskey was harsh after the beer he'd had earlier, and he winced as the amber liquid tipped down his throat. Greed. Greed was what led him here. He'd been thinking more about Casey in the last few days, about his decisions that had led the family to here.

He wished he could take it back, he really did. But now was not the time to be divulging that to anyone. The police were still around, and word in town was that the Sydney cop's famous partner had arrived. He'd seen photos of him on the news a few years back, he knew he'd be a wily bastard. Casey told him he was from Milford, a little farming town down near the border, so he guessed he'd be smarter than most of the cops who were here already, most of them were from the city.

***

The Smith property was a dead end. The carport and sheds were empty, and the place looked deserted. Joanna managed to find a contact for them online and left a message and an email for them to contact her, but Nick advised her that it didn't seem like they were going to be involved in any way.

Nick drove towards Moroco and Joanna sat in the passenger seat. The medication he'd been having to settle the headaches that were coming and going was strong and he could feel his eyes drooping as the afternoon sun bounced off the bonnet and into his face.

'You alright?' Joanna asked.

'Yeah. Been a long day.'

'I can drive if you need?'

Nick shook his head, 'Nah. All good.'

He wasn't sure whether it was being back in the bush, or the sight of the Gabinda Hotel as they drove past it, but it got him thinking about his drinking. It had now been a few months since his last one, and he didn't find himself craving it anymore. He wondered whether the coma had been like a detox for his body, like the one heavy drug users had. He wondered if he'd ever drink again, *Probably,* he thought.

'Moroco is out the main highway to the north,' Joanna pointed. 'About ten ks out.'

They continued on the highway and Nick looked across the open expanse. It looked like it was going to be a good year for the farmers. Moroco's wheat crop was growing well and looked to be only a few weeks away from starting harvest. He smiled at a forgotten memory, one of sitting beside his father in a giant header that cut the wheat, and the other tractor with the back trailer called the mother bin, following closely beside them to pick up the valuable grain.

The entrance to Moroco was impressive. Two long vintage red clinker brick walls had been built and black wrought iron gates stood open. The left wall had a sign painted on it with the word 'Moroco', and then underneath, 'Home of the Blackwood family'. Nick looked down the long, well-maintained driveway. *If you've seen one, you've seen 'em all,* he thought as they continued towards the homestead in the distance. He slowed as the main road came to a fork and he parked next to a single towering palm tree that looked to form the start of the parking area.

The homestead was a single storey home, made of old stone and mud rock back in the 1800s, capped off with what looked like a brand-new corrugated iron roof. A verandah wrapped right around the property that was shaded by the single giant palm tree and a row of jacarandas that blossomed with beautiful purple flowers. There was a wire fence around the front yard and Joanna opened the gate and they walked on through onto the well-maintained front lawn. Somebody was sitting out on the front porch and Nick made a calculated guess it was John Blackwood.

When he stood, the man was tall. He wore a light green button up work shirt. His work jeans were worn and dirty. He wore a well-worn black Akubra hat and bare feet as he walked across the lawn in their direction. 'Afternoon, Joanna,' he said.

'Hi John,' Joanna replied. 'Thought we'd come out to give our condolences.' She pointed to Nick. 'This is my partner, Detective Sergeant Nick Vada. Nick, meet John Blackwood.'

Nick shook his hand. His grip was not soft, but not too firm either. He struck Nick as one of those wily blokes who could fit in in any setting. His teeth were white and straight. Nick spied an expensive watch on his wrist as well. *You can't always hide wealth,* he thought to himself.

'Thank you, Joanna. We appreciate that. Pleasure to meet you, Detective,' John said with a smile. 'Seen you on the telly a while back. Looks like the cops have brought out the big guns.'

Nick smiled. 'We're just here to try and find your family some answers,' Nick replied.

'That would be good, Detective.' He waved them over to the outdoor table on the front verandah. 'Come over, let's get out of this bloody sun. Been in it all day.'

Nick pointed out into the paddocks that surrounded them. 'You must be close to harvest?' he asked. 'A heap of rain coming next week though, once that dries out you'll be good to go.'

John turned back to Nick. 'You're from Milford, I hear? You got land back there?'

Nick shook his head. 'Nah. Family grew up around farms, though. Dad was a shearer.'

'Good man.' The screen door opened and a short woman with dark brown hair walked out. She was wearing neat moleskins and a loose-fitting white shirt. Nick could see her face was red and her eyes were puffy, and he immediately assumed he was looking at Matty's mother. 'Detective, meet my daughter, Gabby.'

Gabby walked over and shook his hand before giving Joanna a rather long hug. He watched the interaction closely and the warmth that Joanna showed to her. He wondered if he could ever be like that as a detective, his approach was certainly a lot more hands off. The screen door opened again and the group turned towards it. A tall man with a prominent tribal tattoo that ran up his neck and right to his jawline, came walking out. His face was a mess, his left eye was half shut and an angry purple bruise ran up the side of his face. He sensed Joanna tense beside him and his radar was on high alert, this guy was clearly bad news.

'Where have you been?' Joanna asked the man.

John turned back to Nick at the stand-off between them. 'This is my brother-in-law Cameron, Nick. Matty's father.'

'G'day,' Cameron muttered in his direction.

Nick had gathered as much. 'I'll reiterate what my partner asked, Cameron. Your son has been found deceased, and you've been missing for two weeks. And now you're here.' He pointed to his face. 'And then there's that. You mind telling us what happened to you?'

Cameron shrugged in a non-committal type of way. 'Got in a blue a few towns over. None of your business really.'

'It's my job to make all of this my business, mate. Unless you don't want me to find out what happened to your son?'

Cameron opened his mouth and Gabby placed her hand on his shoulder to stop him from speaking. 'We want that more than anything, Detective,' she answered.

'Good,' Nick said. He looked to Joanna. She knew this family better than he did, he wanted to watch and listen. 'Joanna?'

'You'll need to provide us some evidence of where you've been Cameron. Anything like photos, receipts, calls you made, people you saw. If you don't, we could get a search warrant.'

'You won't need to do that,' John replied. 'He'll get that information for you, won't you Cameron?'

Cameron looked like a deer in the headlights. Something was up. Nick just wasn't quite sure what yet. He needed to look into Cameron's past and his rap sheet, see if he had any prior convictions that would make him good for it. He found it hard to believe a father could do that to his child. But he had seen the worst of the worst, so he wouldn't have been surprised.

'Gabby, we'll need you to formally identify the body,' Joanna said calmly. 'He's been taken to Dubbo right now for an autopsy and you are more than welcome to make your way there if that would be possible?'

Tears streamed from Gabby's face as she nodded defiantly. 'Yep. I want to see him one last time anyway.'

'Good, good.' Joanna patted her hand gently. The next question was going to be trickier. 'Now preliminary thoughts in our investigation are that he was held. For an extended period of time, obviously. He was still in the same clothes from the night he went missing.'

'God,' Cameron said, as he put his head into his hands.

'We think he's been held somewhere. But for now we don't have any more information. Can any of you at this table think of why anyone would want to hold him? What did they stand to gain?'

'What about Carl Lucivi?' John Blackwood said, pointing back towards the town. 'Bloke's a paedo. Always has been. I've seen him skulking around the kids' pool in the summer. Bloke is bad news.'

Joanna shook her head. 'I've already spoken to Carl. He was in Sydney the night of the rodeo.'

The group fell silent and Nick turned to John Blackwood. 'What about Neville Ford and his bull riders?'

John's face turned sour. 'I've never liked bloody Neville Ford. Bloke's a tosser. But I don't have any issues with his riders, though.'

Nick wondered why, and went to speak on that when Joanna spoke suddenly. 'What do you do for work Gabby?'

Gabby turned to her with a questioning gaze. 'I work on the reception at Doctor McGee's office in town, why do you ask?'

'Didn't you say you were a nurse?' Joanna asked. 'Remember when we met? The night of the rodeo. You said you were a nurse?'

Gabby blinked twice and her mouth opened and then closed. 'I lied. What can I say?'

'Why?' Joanna asked.

Gabby looked down at the table. 'It's silly really. Your brother Benji. we dated years ago for a short while. I was just trying to make myself sound a bit more important than I really am.'

'Okay then,' Joanna replied. Nick watched her, she didn't seem convinced.

Nick stored that comment away for a later date. 'Alright then, we are going to be in town for the next week. Cameron, we are going to have to find some time to have a chat over the next few days. With you too, John. C'mon Jo, let's leave these guys in peace for now. Have a good night, everyone.'

Nick could see that Gabby didn't seem up for much more questioning. Going to ID Matty would be hard enough, they didn't need to push her this early until after that.

Chapter Twenty-Six

Joanna sat in the passenger seat as Nick drove back towards town. The sun was setting, casting brilliant orange and purple light across the horizon. Her mind raced. Cameron Parsons being back in the picture was an interesting spanner thrown in the works. He looked like he'd been bashed. But why, she wondered. They needed to check his alibis.

She stole a glance at her partner. He had been good out there. His old self. It felt good to have him back, to have them back working a case together. It felt like the last few months had never happened. 'What did you think about all that?' she asked him.

He kept his eyes on the road. 'Odd. Really odd. The partner just goes missing for a few weeks and it's all happy families? Something doesn't feel right.'

'I agree.'

'We'll need to check up on his alibi. Get the Sergeant involved, she seems pretty switched on. She might have better contacts with the locals a few towns over.' *Smart thinking*, Joanna thought. Sometimes the locals got their backs up when the Sydney cops started asking questions. 'Hopefully Troy gets back to us tonight or tomorrow morning. They should have done the autopsy by now. Chief put a hurry up on it. Surprised Bec wasn't out here. The Chief would've wanted the best.'

What an odd comment to make, Joanna thought. Bec Ranijan, Nick's ex-girlfriend, was a crime scene technician when they had met. She'd since moved into an office role and wasn't on the road anymore. Nick knew that though; she remembered them having that conversation. 'Bec's in support now, isn't she?' Joanna asked. 'Office role.'

'Oh yeah,' Nick replied slowly. 'I need to call her,' he added.

'Don't think we'll be getting an invite to that wedding,' Joanna said with a laugh.

Nick turned to her. 'Wedding? What? Is Bec getting married?'

Joanna turned to him and could see a genuine look of shock. She wasn't sure how to reply. The Chief had said there may be some short-term memory loss, but this was more significant. And news that she knew had upset him. She treaded lightly.

'Yeah. We spoke about it in Blarnie, on our last case, remember? Some lawyer from Coogee.'

'Coogee,' Nick spoke slowly. 'Oh yeah. That's right.'

They both fell silent and Joanna wasn't sure whether he remembered or if he was lying. She eyed her watch, it was 6:30 pm and the day had already been a long one. She worried about Nick, maybe this was all too soon. 'Hey, what do you say we call it? It's a thirty-minute drive out the other side of town to the Ford's.'

'I'm easy,' Nick replied.

Joanna's phone rang. 'Hey, sis,' Benji said. 'How's it going?'

Joanna sighed. 'It's been a day.'

'I bet. I was wondering if you wanted to do dinner tonight? Pub?'

Joanna smiled. Perfect timing. She looked across at Nick. 'Benji's inviting us out for dinner to the pub. You interested?' Nick nodded along. 'Alright, give us an hour, we'll meet you there?'

'Deal.'

***

For a Thursday night, the pub was busy. Joanna and Nick took the same table she had sat at with her brother a few weeks earlier and looked at the menus. They hadn't eaten lunch and she was starving. Nick took her order and walked off to grab some drinks while she sat and waited.

She spied Glenn's red Dodge Ram pull into the carpark and she tried to see the occupants inside. She had kept in touch with the cowboy but knew it was more out of loneliness than anything else. He had been a good conversationalist on the quiet nights back home in her apartment, and at that time she had wondered if she was ever going to see him again.

But it wasn't Glenn climbing out of the driver's seat, it was Benji, along with another man she couldn't quite make out until he got closer. She couldn't believe her eyes, it was Bryce, the young man who had been stabbed by the bull horn on her first night in town. He was tall and thin and was dressed all in black, and wearing a black Akubra hat. The only thing that wasn't black was the white neck brace that sat on his shoulders and held his head upright. Nick sat back down beside her and placed a beer in front of her. She eyed his glass; he'd ordered a lemon squash, which she hadn't been expecting. She pointed out to the carpark. 'Remember how I told you about the rider who got injured?'

'Yeah,' Nick replied.

'That's him.'

Benji walked up the ramp onto the deck with Bryce in tow. They were both smiling, happy to have surprised her, she could tell. 'Hey, sis. Look who I brought along.'

Bryce shook her hand and then Nick's. Joanna hadn't realised it at the time but it was even more prominent now as she saw Bryce up close, he was just a kid. His face was still badly bruised around his eye sockets and his nose was yellow. She could just make out the staining of antiseptic cream above his neck brace from where his wounds would be. He removed his hat and spoke in a voice so low it was almost a whisper. 'I just wanted to thank you for that night. If you and Gabby Blackwood hadn't been there, I don't know what would have happened.'

Joanna had to lean in to hear him. She placed her hand on his shoulder. 'It's no worries at all. I'm sure if I wasn't around Benji would have sorted you out though.'

'He got out of hospital yesterday,' Benji said. 'Told me he wanted to come straight to the pub.'

'Can you drink?' Joanna asked him.

He shook his head. 'No.' He held up a small tube. 'I've got a feeding tube for the next few months. Just wanted to be somewhere where there were people. Isolation in a hospital room can do crazy things to people.'

Joanna looked at Benji with her best motherly glare. Bryce was in no state to be coming to a pub and he knew it. She wanted him to know she wasn't happy.

'I get that,' Nick said, replying to Bryce's whispers. 'I've just got out myself.'

Benji turned. 'Shit, sorry! Nick, I'm Benji, Joanna's brother, and this is Bryce.'

Nick shook both of their hands. 'Nice to meet you boys. Joanna has told me a lot about you.' Joanna knew that was a lie. She was always cagey about her family. She had told Nick a little bit about her dad when they first met, but that was it. Even less was said about her brother. But she appreciated the gesture. He held his squash up towards Bryce. 'I read a news article about your accident. It said you were riding a bull called Bandsaw. No relation to Chainsaw, is it?'

Bryce smiled wide at the statement, it seemed Nick knew his bulls. Joanna wondered if there was anything he didn't know about the bush. She felt like he'd probably forgotten more than she would ever know.

Benji answered for him. 'Yep. Direct relation. One of the meanest bastards we have at the moment.'

Nick whistled. 'Bloody impressive, mate. Wish I had have seen it.'

'He got past eight seconds too,' Benji added. 'Poor bastard was robbed. I reckon the judges were too busy throwin' up their dinners when the horn went in him, to be worried about scoring him.'

'Why eight seconds?' Joanna asked.

'Scoring only begins after eight seconds,' Benji replied.

'I'll be back, though,' Bryce whispered. 'I'll show 'em.'

Joanna liked his enthusiasm but didn't totally agree with him. She wasn't his wife or mother though, he was a grown man and he could do whatever he wanted.

The mood was lowered when Benji asked, 'So, how did today go? You don't have to say too much if you can't.'

Joanna trusted her brother. And she thought he could be helpful when it came to their investigation. She knew Nick wouldn't mind if she told him some information. 'Look it wasn't great. He was found in the Smith's dam. I'm sure that's common knowledge by now.'

Benji sipped from his drink. 'Yeah, we heard that. Poor little bugger. I just can't imagine how or why anyone would want to do that. And poor Gabby. I need to give her a call.'

'He was still in his clothes from the rodeo,' Nick added. Joanna hadn't been sure if they were meant to divulge that or not. But knew if the Blackwoods and Cameron Parsons knew, then it may soon get out anyway.

'Jesus,' Bryce said as he sipped his beer.

'We think he must have been held somewhere over the last few weeks. Kept captive. Until the moment they decided to kill him.'

'But why?' Benji asked. 'To upset Gabby? For money? Or something worse?'

'We don't know,' Joanna said. 'Odd that his phone was found so close to Neville's farm though,'

'And his body,' Nick added. 'John Blackwood said he doesn't get along with Neville Ford. What's the backstory there?'

Their dinners were placed in front of them and Joanna eyed the giant steak she'd ordered. She'd made the right choice. The pub was full now as patrons drank and laughed on the front deck. The night was warm and the beers were going down a treat. She looked across at Nick drinking his lemon squash, and had to smile to herself. It was odd seeing him not drink, but she guessed in a weird way, she preferred it. Maybe he could look after her for once, instead of the other way around.

Benji bit off a big mouthful of his chicken schnitzel and answered her question. 'Weird one all that. Was a bit before my time.'

'Do you know anything at all?' she asked.

Benji looked over his shoulder for some reason, like what he was about to say would be incriminating to someone. 'Well, rumour has it that when Casey Blackwood was a young bloke, Neville caught him selling some real dodgy pain meds to some of the rookie cowboys. Neville found out about it and lost his shit. Went out to the Blackwood farm and accused the whole family of being drug dealers. Which John Blackwood of course took major offence to. All his help and funding that used to go into the rodeo circuit got pulled after that. He hasn't spoken to Neville since.'

Joanna drank from her beer and smiled. Some cases came together quickly, and some took longer, but this was interesting, very interesting, and it gave her and Nick something to go on with.

Chapter Twenty-Seven

Casey drove along the connecting farm road between Moroco and Riverleigh and stared out into the distance. He couldn't believe his father had made the call to let Cameron Parsons go. It was an idiotic decision, and one that could put the whole farm in jeopardy.

His father had been off for a few weeks now, he could see it. He could see it in his body language, his posture and his demeanour. Something was eating at his dad and he didn't know what it was. He wondered now if it was grief; the grief that he felt for his dead grandson. But he pushed those thoughts aside. Young Matty had spent some time with them on the farm as he grew up but not a lot. He was a reserved, quiet kid, happy to spend his afternoons engrossed on his phone or Nintendo Switch, unable to show much interest in heading outside with his grandfather and uncle. He'd be surprised if his dad was showing emotion about that; he'd never shown any grief before, not even when their mother died when he was a kid.

He thought about the operation, and the amount of heat that was currently in the town with the police poking around. It was inexplicable why anybody would want to kill Matty. Killing him gained nothing, only pain and sadness for their family. He wished he could find the killer before the police did. He would've shown him what real pain was.

The next morning he sat at his kitchen dining table with a coffee in hand and a newspaper open on the table. His wife had taken his daughter into town to do some shopping. He stood up when he heard a car turn up outside, curious as to who would be visiting him at that time of the morning. He looked out the window and saw his sister's small black hatchback nose into the carport beside the house. She got out and locked it, putting her keys into her pocket as she walked over the front lawn. He chuckled to himself. She'd turned into a real townie.

He walked to his back sliding door as she stepped onto the porch. 'Morning.'

She walked into the living and dining area and looked around. He realised she wouldn't have been there since they had the place renovated. 'Morning. This is nice,' she said. 'Really nice.'

'Thanks. You want a coffee?'

'Sure.'

He walked on into their kitchen and started making a coffee from their new coffee machine. His wife had worked at the local coffee shop a few towns over when she was younger and was a master. He was still learning and hoped he wouldn't mess it up. 'Latte with regular milk? That's all I've got in my repertoire at the moment.'

Gabby blinked. 'Fine by me.'

The coffee machine hissed and whirred, and he watched his sister as he packed the ground coffee beans into the handle before placing it into the machine. She looked better than she had the day before, but still a shadow of her usual bubbly self. After he steamed the milk, he poured it into a mug and placed it in front of her before sitting down. 'How are you holding up?'

She held the cup up to her nose and sniffed it. 'These beans are from in town, aren't they? Dave's shop?'

He nodded, well aware she was trying to shy away from the question, but he insisted. 'They are. I'll ask again. How are you holding up?'

She shrugged. 'I'm okay. Empty is the word, I guess. I don't know where I'm supposed to go from here.'

'You've just got to take it one day at a time, Gab.' He was unsure what else he could say that could make it any better.

'The police called this morning. The autopsy is done, so we can go and see him now.' A single tear ran down her left cheek and she wiped it away. 'We'll go and get him. Dads organised the McKay's funeral home to bring him home.'

Casey knew the owner, David McKay. He was an old family friend. He had organised their mother's funeral with little to no input from their father. He remembered it like it was yesterday. All of the people, giving their condolences, most he had never seen again. Vultures, his Dad had called them all at the time. His father's disdain for people only grew worse as he got older, he realised.

Casey had a mountain of jobs to do that day but knew he had to be there for his sister. Nothing else mattered in that moment; their falling out years ago had to be left in the past. 'What can I do to help? Do you want me to come with you?'

Gabby sipped from her cup and shook her head. 'Cameron said no. He doesn't want you or Dad there.'

Casey stiffened in his seat. 'Alright then.'

Gabby looked him in the eyes. 'What is going on with Dad? I can tell something is up. What aren't you both telling me?'

Casey opened his mouth and then closed it again. He thought for a short moment, and then disregarded the idea. 'Nothing's going on. He lost his grandson; he's entitled to be a little bit off isn't he?'

Gabby scoffed at that. 'Off? He never put in any effort with Matty! You lot all out here,' she pointed around at his home. 'Living in luxury while we lived in that old dump in town! All because he didn't agree on who my partner was. You both gave up the right to be upset for my little family when you gave up on me years ago!'

Casey felt like he'd been slapped in the face. She was right, of course, but he wasn't going to admit it. He stood up. She was upset, and he wasn't going to fight with her on a day like this. Not on the day she was bringing her dead boy home. 'I'm not going to fight with you, Gab. Whatever you and Dad had going on back then was out of my hands. I went away to school and came back to this. If you ever need me to help with anything, let me know.' He walked to the sink and tipped the remainder of his cold coffee out. 'If you don't, the door's over there.'

Gabby pushed her coffee cup away and stood up. She tucked her hair behind her ears. 'If you won't tell me what's going on with Dad, I'll find out. And if it has anything to do with my son going missing, there's going to be hell to pay. See you later.'

***

Troy, the crime scene technician, finished his report on his laptop beside the body of Matty Blackwood. It was all pretty self-explanatory and he wondered if his information would help Nick and Joanna in any way. The boy had been strangled to death, his initial reporting had been correct on that. What was interesting was the fact that the finger marks on his neck meant that he had been facing away from his attacker during the strangulation, this implied that perhaps he was known in some way to his attacker, or at least his attacker felt some kind of remorse for what he did; that's what the detectives would say.

The only thing he was waiting on before he spoke to the detectives was a tox screen report. He'd sent the blood samples as express priority to the laboratory that morning and expected a phone call any minute before he could press send on the report. He expected nothing untoward, child victims were rarely intoxicated or had anything in their system, it was usually their killers who had that issue. The results for the unidentified matter came back on his shoes and Nick Vada had been right: it was cow manure.

Troy's partner, Lucy, walked through the morgue doors, a clipboard in hand. 'Nearly done?'

He pulled down his mask and slid over on the chair towards the computer closest to her. He had been divorced a few years back and he wasn't always sure how to read the signs with women, but the way his younger partner looked and spoke to him sometimes made him pause. He was smart though, and liked to think he was professional. He was never going to make the first move. He'd never been one to do it before and wasn't going to start now.

'Just about. Waiting on the tox screen report to come back and I can finalise the report.'

Lucy looked at her watch. 'When will we head back to Sydney?'

'Tomorrow if they don't need anything else from us.'

She pulled out her phone. 'I thought that might be the case.' She turned her screen to show him an image of a local Chinese restaurant. 'I booked a table here for 7pm. Did you want to do dinner?'

He smiled. Her perfume smelled great and he could tell she had recently washed her hair, it had a certain smell about it that he loved. 'Sounds good to me.'

'Great,' she replied. 'I'm going to head back to the motel to freshen up if you're okay here?'

'Yeah, I'm all good.'

She walked out through the double doors. Sometimes this job wasn't always doom and gloom. An alert pinged on his laptop and he saw it was the laboratory. *Great*, he thought, he could press send on this report now and get the all clear before heading out to dinner.

He opened the report and his mouth fell open as he read. 'Sample types, blood, urine and gastric contents –Victim had 100mg/L oxycodone in his bloodstream, which is a toxic amount. Taken orally this can cause respiratory depression. This amount alone can be enough to cause coma-like symptoms and a high chance of death. Victim also has trace amounts of fentanyl, codeine and morphine.'

Chapter Twenty-Eight

The path was dark and barely illuminated. Only the faintest glimmer of moonlight shone through as he sprinted between the thick trees. He didn't know what he was running towards, or why, he just knew he had to stop whatever it was before it hurt again. He reached a fork in the path and he had to make a decision. Something in his mind told him to go left and he followed his gut. He sprinted around the last fork in the road and felt for his gun. It was at that moment he realised he didn't have it. He had come to a stop in a clearing, and as much as he willed his feet to move, he was rooted to the spot. A disembodied voice from the darkness whispered, 'Help me, Nick.' But there was nothing he could do. The figure rose slowly from thin air, a black shadow with shining red eyes. The shadow suddenly lurched towards him and he jumped with a start and opened his eyes.

A ceiling fan circled overhead in his motel room, trying in vain to circulate the warm air in his room. He fumbled for the split system remote on his bedside table and turned the air conditioner fan on to its highest setting. He knew it was going to be a hot one the next day.

The dream was always the same, and it had been happening since he woke after his coma. He had read the police report about what happened at Blarnie; it was one of the first things he did when he got out of hospital. He still didn't remember anything from his time in the town but didn't want the Chief to know that, so he'd read up on every detail, and tried to put as much of it in his memory bank as he could to cover himself. He assumed the dream was some sort of coping mechanism for the trauma he had gone through - well that's what his therapist had told him. He didn't believe in any of those things. Bad things happened to good people, it was the way life went sometimes; you couldn't plan for it, all you could do was work through those things and keep moving forward. Everyone's luck would turn eventually.

***

Last night, for the first time in a long time, he had left the pub just as it seemed like the fun was about to begin. Amelia the sergeant had turned up to join the crew and Nick had left her and Joanna sitting at a table, deep in conversation with wines in hand. In all honesty, he didn't think he could stomach much more lemon squash and his head was beginning to ache with the loud music anyway, so he wished them all goodnight.

He had returned to his room and began researching. Joanna had been meticulous the night of the disappearance, in nearly thirty-minute intervals she had pulled her phone out and snapped as many images of what she was seeing in front of her at that very moment. These had proved invaluable to him as he used these images to take himself back to the night Matty disappeared. He looked through images of the near empty stands, and the stragglers who seemed content in watching the night away from their seats. He saw the rides in the showground alley, the big favourites that were at every show and the young kids and teenagers standing around getting ready for their next adrenaline hit. The food court was in the next batch of photos, and he looked through the images of the people in the crowd, all still unaware that anything had gone wrong.

The final batch of photos were from the morning after. From the mud map Joanna had given him of the showgrounds from that night, he could see the location of where Matty's hat had fallen on the edge of Barnes Road. It was a short distance to the national highway, which went in two directions, one way to Sydney and one way to Adelaide. He had opened a map of the region and traced that major highway away towards the next corresponding town. Moroco, the Blackwood's farm boundary ran right along that route. He noted that down for further investigation. Joanna's photos of the next morning were of the rodeo crews' trailers, cars, utes and caravans. He spied a giant motorhome close to the arena, a fifth wheeler like the ones you saw in America, then four rows across from it was a giant red stock crate with a 'Beef Bus' sticker on the back of it. His mind tried to grasp at an idea, and he stared at the photo for another moment before the thought disappeared. He looked at the time and decided to call it a night. He wanted to be fresh for the next day.

***

In the morning he slowly peeled himself out of bed and had a long hot shower. He let the water run over him for a lot longer than usual. His brain felt like it had a thin layer of fog inside it. The medication was helping, he knew that, but he wondered how much longer this was going to last. He needed to speak with the specialist in the next week or two anyway and tried to make a mental note to ask him. He climbed out of the shower and dressed for the day. He grabbed his worn tan Akubra from on top of the TV. He was going to speak to cowboys today, so he needed to look the part.

He walked down to Joanna's room and knocked on the door. 'It's open,' came her voice from inside.

He pushed the door open and stopped. Joanna was lying on her stomach in a sports bra and shorts. She was stretching out her lower back in an intricate yoga position. 'Ah, sorry, I'll give you five.'

Joanna laughed. 'Sit down. It's only a sports bra, surely you've seen worse.'

He cleared his throat and pulled out the single chair next to the table, he kept his eyes looking downward but snuck a peak at the ab muscles on her stomach, she looked like she was getting fitter than he'd ever seen before. 'I spent the night going through your photos. Very thorough.'

She laughed again. 'I could get used to this new Nick.'

'New Nick?' he replied.

'Yeah. You're the one usually pissed at the pub and I'm the one back in the room doing the research.' She stopped when she saw the look on his face. 'Sorry. I overstepped my mark there.'

He held up both hands with a smile. 'Nah, that's fair you got me. You've got a point.'

She stood up and stretched her arms over her head. 'What do you think about what Benji said last night? About Casey Blackwood?'

'It's interesting. The Blackwoods don't strike me as being involved in anything like that. And going by what Benji said, it was years ago. He looks like he's grown up a bit since then.'

'Benji reckons Casey basically runs Moroco these days. John's taken a step back.'

'Makes sense. Even though farming sounds basic, the methods are constantly evolving and changing. I've seen many farms die because their owners couldn't get with the times. John seems smarter than most; getting Casey involved early is a good call.'

Once Joanna was ready to start the day, they headed straight to the Gabinda police station. Nick wanted to ask the Inspector what he knew about any drug dealing in the town and he headed for the office while Joanna stopped to speak with the Sergeant.

The Inspector had the local newspaper spread across his desk. 'Morning Detective. How's it all going?'

Nick observed the newspaper, the two dirty plates and empty cups near the drawers and the dust on his shelves. This cop was over it, he could tell. 'The cue's in the rack,' one of his old sergeants used to say about cops who were months away from retiring. He hoped he could at least help them get answers here. 'It's going,' he replied.

'Amelia tells me Cameron Parsons is back in town. Went walkabout, I assume?'

'Something like that. We'll need to check up on where he's been. Shouldn't be too difficult, he's banged up pretty badly. Looks like he's had a flogging. Said he was in a bar fight.'

'Hmm.'

Nick watched the Inspector closely. His disinterest was clear. 'I wanted to ask you about something else. About Casey Blackwood.'

'What about him?'

'Heard that Neville Ford had a bit of a blow up at him back in the day? That he and the Blackwood family don't get along?'

The Inspector pushed his glasses up on the end of his nose and leaned back in the chair. 'What are you saying, Detective? That you think Neville Ford is somehow involved in all of this? Neville Ford's a good man.'

Nick took a seat across from him. 'Not insinuating anything. I'm just asking questions. All of these incidents from the past could lead to something, or nothing at all. But it's our job to dig.'

'Alright, alright. I get it.' He sipped from his coffee cup. 'It was years ago by the way. Long before I ran this place. I was a sergeant at the time, I was the one that took the call and went out there.'

Nick turned as Joanna sat down beside him and listened in. 'You were there?'

'I was. Neville Ford called me, furious. Said he wanted me out there to sort out an issue so I drove out with a constable who's long gone and spoke with him. He said he caught Casey Blackwood at the bunkhouse selling oxycodone to a few of his riders. He even had a box of them he gave to us back then, all looked legit.'

'What happened when he caught him?' Joanna asked.

'Nothing really, Neville just had a go at him, told him to get the hell off his property and not come back. He had a row with the riders who were buying it too.'

'Did you investigate any further?'

The Inspector shook his head and shrugged. 'It was the Blackwoods, what was I supposed to do? I drove out to Moroco and had a quiet word with John. He was furious, told me Casey would be appropriately punished, that he was a dumb school kid and he would learn his lesson.'

Chapter Twenty-Nine

Joanna read the email out as they travelled towards the Ford's farm. 'Sample types, blood, urine and gastric contents – Victim had 100mg/L oxycodone is his bloodstream, which is a toxic amount. Taken orally this can cause respiratory depression. This amount alone can be enough to cause coma-like symptoms and most likely death. Victim also has trace amounts of fentanyl, codeine and morphine.'

'They drugged him. The poor little fella didn't stand a chance,' Nick replied.

'Report says his attacker strangled him from behind,' Joanna continued. 'They couldn't face him. Does that mean it was someone he knew?'

'Could be,' Nick replied. 'Or could not. I couldn't imagine anyone feeling super comfortable strangling an eleven-year-old kid.'

'Oxycodone,' Joanna said, repeating the name of the drug that killed Matty.

'Yeah, I thought the same thing,' Nick replied. It was the drug that Casey Blackwood had been selling to the bull riders back when he was a kid. He wondered if there was a connection there. He pulled his car up out front of the two-storey brick home. It had a top floor balcony accessed through two double doors. On the balcony was a green set of table and chairs. A woman sat smoking a cigarette. As Nick and Joanna got out of the car she yelled out, 'Help you?'

Nick held his badge up. 'We're detectives with the New South Wales police. Hoping we could speak to Neville Ford?'

She inhaled on her cigarette and let the smoke slowly come out of her nose. She pointed away from the home. 'He's down at the arena. He doesn't spend much time up at the house.'

'Thanks.' They got back in the car and continued on towards a fork in the dirt road. In the distance to the left was a giant shed that stood out against the vast blue sky. Nick continued along to the left and eventually parked beside the shed next to Glenn's red Dodge Ram ute. They got out and looked at the giant shed. It was a light grey and had an enormous sliding barn door like an aeroplane hangar. They could hear voices and cheers from inside and they walked towards the opening to investigate.

The area seemed even bigger from the inside. Nick estimated it to be at least two football fields long. The far end held pens and small round fenced off areas for horses, and closer to them was a full pro bull riding arena. The fencing even had the sponsor signage like the stuff he'd seen on TV. To the left of the arena was a path that ran the length of the whole shed and against the back wall was a row of metal bleachers that towered above them.

Joanna whistled. 'They could have had the rodeo here. It's massive.'

Nick stepped forward onto the path and they made their way towards the action. There was a staircase that travelled upwards and connected to an overhead metal gantry looking over the arena. Standing up on top of the gantry looking down at the arena was a bunch of men, and Nick recognised Benji among them.

'Joanna! Nick! Come up here,' Benji yelled out.

They climbed up the steep staircase on the stainless checker plated deck. There were metal handrails either side and Nick watched Joanna grip the one on the left tightly. 'Don't tell me you're afraid of heights,' he said.

She turned around and gave him a foul look. 'I wouldn't say I'm a fan of them.'

They walked along the gantry to the group of men. Nick knew Benji, but wasn't able to place the rest of the men. They were all cowboys though, that was for sure. Two of them including Benji wore the padded leather vests that all bull riders were sanctioned to wear. One of the other men was dressed up more than the rest. He wore cream moleskins. His R.M.Williams boots were polished to a high shine and his hair was slicked back neatly. He was who Nick assumed they were looking for.

'Neville Ford.' The elderly farm owner extended his hand and Nick shook it. Nick eyed the bent fingers and the deep scar across the top of his hand. This was an old bloke who could tell a story or two.

'Detective Sergeant Nick Vada,' he replied. 'And you've met my partner, Joanna Gray?'

'I have,' Neville said with a warm smile in her direction. 'Vada you said? Was your father Tim Vada?'

'Yeah,' he replied, unsure how the man knew that.

Neville patted him on the shoulder. 'I knew your old fella back when we I was a young bloke. He drove a mother bin for a harvest for us up in Queensland on one of the farms I worked at. Only remember it because of his last name. Was a bit unusual.'

Nick looked at Joanna. He was dumbfounded. His father hadn't ventured out much from Milford, but he did know that during a trying time in the droughts of the early 90s he was forced up towards Queensland during the harvest months to make ends meet for their family. His father had never said much about those days, so it was fascinating to hear that he had been remembered by someone.

'Seriously?' He laughed. 'What are the odds? I remember when I was a young fella that Dad had to venture up that way.'

'Yeah, he was a hard worker, your old man. Dedicated, my old boss used to call him. Would work, have a beer and a feed, and sleep. Was like a clock you could set him to. Never caused any trouble anywhere. You look a bit like him too.' He chuckled. 'Although you are a bit taller.'

'Yeah. I got that from my mum,' Nick replied. He already felt comfortable around the old farmer; he rarely spoke of his mother in public.

Neville rolled up one of his shirt sleeves. 'He still around? Send him my regards if you could? Tell him Nev said g'day.'

'He passed, sorry to say. Lung cancer.'

Neville shook his head. 'Sorry to hear that. The bloke didn't mind a smoke back in the day. That's what I say to Wendy, my missus. They'll bloody catch up to ya!'

'Neville, do you mind if we had a quiet word?' Joanna asked. 'In private.'

Neville looked across at her. 'Sure. Come down into my office. Got AC in there.'

They left the three men on the gantry and followed Neville down the opposite staircase. On this side of the giant shed was a long single storey brick building built against the side wall. Neville pointed as he spoke. 'Got some locker rooms for the training riders through there. Showers. Dunnies. Even got a little kitchen and room for them to rest between sessions when need be.' He stopped next to two doors. 'Left side is first aid.' He chuckled, 'That one gets a fair bit of use. Lucky Wendy's pretty good at fixin' up whoever gets hurt.' He pointed to the door on the right and then opened it, ushering them through in front of him. 'And this last one is my office.'

Nick didn't know what to expect but was surprised to see a tastefully modern interior. There was a woodgrain desk with a chair and laptop, a couch and sofa chair along with a giant row of big screen TVs across the back wall with world clocks above them.

'This is where I do all my drafting,' Neville said.

'Drafting?' Joanna asked.

'Yeah. I keep an eye on all the big circuits. Pro Bull Riding, or the PBR tour, that being the biggest. US, Canada, Brazil and now us. Any names I see a future with who aren't getting a chance, I try and get out here. Anyone injured I'll try and get them out here and get them rehabbed. Some of these young guns are bringing in big money now. Social media has changed things. Young Bryce is one of my most promising young riders. He's got thousands of followers on his platforms. Followers means sponsors, and sponsors means more revenue for all of us.' He held his arms out wide open. 'And I can keep the lights on.'

Nick was surprised. He'd pictured a weathered old bull rider stuck in the past. But Neville was sharp as a tack. And it sounded like he was keeping up with the times. Nick didn't need to wonder how he'd manage to build a place like this, he could see it now; he was a smart man.

Nick started. 'Neville, I can see you're a busy man so we won't keep you long. We only have a few questions to ask, and you don't strike me as a bullshitter.'

Neville sat down in his office chair and placed both of his leather boots on his desk with a smile. 'Straight to the point like your old man. He never beat around the bush.'

'Have you seen or heard anything untoward around here since the rodeo? Any reason why you think that Matty Blackwood's body would be found so close to your property?'

'That I do not know,' Neville replied. 'The poor little bugger. It's bloody odd though. The phone and now the poor boy. On the Smith farm too, I can't understand why anybody would want to take him.'

'You'd be willing to let us have a chat with the men here? And have a look around the property?' Nick stopped. He realised how he sounded, and what he was insinuating. 'I'm not implying anything, I just take you as a stand-up bloke, and any help you could give would be much appreciated.'

'Of course. My doors are open. Do anything you need, Detective.'

It was a good start, Nick thought. 'John Blackwood,' he said.

'What about him?'

'We want to know why you and John Blackwood had a falling out years ago. Could you explain what that was all about?'

Neville rubbed his chin. 'Shit. That was long, long time ago. But yeah, sure. My boys were all having a rough year. We were full to the brim with injured blokes, like I'd never seen before. Probably my fault, I was pushin' 'em bloody hard back then. I wanted them to be the best. Anyway, I noticed a change in the boys. I could tell straightaway something was up. Miraculous recoveries from bad injuries. Broken arms and the like and they're back on the bull in a week. Never seen anything like it. Then I started noticing a couple of blokes out of it, ya know? Sleeping in the bleachers during the day. Not even turning up. It was Wendy who found out first. She found a pack of pills in one of the rider's pockets. Knew it wasn't anything we'd given them.' He sipped from a mug on the desk. 'We're legit here, Detective. If you're injured you go to Dubbo to the doctors and get set right. I don't condone anything illegal here. Easy way to lose sponsors.'

'And John Blackwood?'

'Ah, yes. I'm getting to that. Anyway, young Casey Blackwood started hanging around here a lot. I asked him if he was keen on learning how to ride and he said no. I had a bad feeling about him, ya know? I spoke to Wendy about it and she agreed something was up.'

'So what did you do about it?'

'One night I was here in my office late, watching old tapes from back in the day. This joint's empty by dark, all the men head back to the bunkhouse or into town or wherever they need. I found Casey Blackwood in the riders lounge, the one just down there, selling to one of the boys. He had a big backpack, it was bloody full to the brim with all sorts of shit. Different types of painkillers, drugs, all the worst shit. All the addictive stuff, and it all clicked. He was selling that shit to my boys and they were all hiked up on painkillers. Half of them off in La La land. I wasn't about to lose every sponsor I had, or worse get locked up in jail. I took the bag off him and threw it in the dumpster out front. Then I called John Blackwood and told him I didn't want any part of his dirty drug-dealing son being out on my farm ever again. Naturally you can imagine how John took that.'

The stories matched up then, Nick thought. 'And who was he selling to that night?' he asked.

Neville chuckled. 'Bloody Cameron Parsons. Ended up shacking up with his sister in the end anyway. Cameron didn't last much longer here.' Neville thought for a short moment. 'And Dean Taranto. He's still around these days. I gave him the bloody dressing down of his life back then. But he's straightened himself out.'

Chapter Thirty

Joanna listened to Neville speak and tried to make sense of what she was hearing. She wondered whether they had gone too deep on this thread. *So what if the Blackwoods and the Fords had a falling out years ago*, she thought. Neville Ford stood to gain nothing in Matty's disappearance.

Cameron Parsons was still an interesting prospect to her, although what he stood to gain again was the biggest question. She had watched him closely every time she'd seen him. She still struggled to find a reason that he could be involved in any way, and he wasn't acting like somebody guilty of murder.

Dean Taranto hadn't struck Joanna as the type of man who would get into trouble with the law but that was only from the very limited interactions she'd had with him. From her memory, he'd been quiet and polite and Benji only had good things to say about him and he'd been quite helpful when looking for Matty's phone on the Smith farm. 'Dean. What's his story?' she asked Neville.

'Came to me when he was a young bloke. I'd say sixteen or seventeen. Dropped out of school. Parents are from up north somewhere. Always wanted to be a bull rider. He was good when he was young. He was in the top three in Australia for a few years there. Did one year on the circuit in the States. Came off a bull in Oklahoma and it stood on his leg and smashed his knee to smithereens. Never was the same after that.'

'And he still rides?' Joanna asked.

Neville chuckled. 'He does. He's more of a sideshow now. He still competes with the big guns but he's just makin' up the numbers. He's nearly forty. Well past his days at the top.'

'And how would money be for him?' Nick asked. It was a smart question, Joanna thought. His mind was tracking in the same direction hers was.

Neville shrugged. 'None of them are that well off. Your brother's doing better than him with prize money at the moment. But he does okay. There's another farmhouse on this property over near my southern boundary that he stays in from time to time. Helps me out on the farm here when it gets busy, and I'll pay him a little bit more. He's been around longer than anyone.'

'And you're sure there is no-one else you can think of who's caused any trouble around here?' Joanna asked.

'No, sorry.'

Nick stood up. 'Thanks Neville. As I said before, no reason why we couldn't look around a little bit before we go?'

'Be my guest,' Neville said.

'Is Dean around?' Joanna asked.

Neville stood up with them. 'Nah, he's headed over to Condobolin. There's a small pre-season rodeo there that some of us go to. I'm heading over there on Friday.'

Joanna got Dean's number and saved it in her phone before Neville led them back towards the arena. There was a man across from them standing on top of the pen gates, with a ferocious looking black bull with wide horns underneath him. Joanna spied Benji out in the arena watching on as they returned to the top of the gantry to see the show.

'I'll give him three seconds,' Neville said to them.

The gate suddenly exploded open and it was nearly timed by Neville to a tee. The bull roared out sideways and the man leaned right to compensate for the spin. What he hadn't allowed for was the rear of the bull kicking up aggressively at the same time and he was launched sideways and down onto the ground in a heap.

Benji and another man shooed the bull into a further pen and then raced to help their friend. He got up gingerly, his pride damaged more than his body, and he tipped his hat to them on the gantry.

'You were right on the money,' Nick said.

Neville winked at him and then yelled down, 'You gotta watch for that back kick, Jesse. Keep your rope hand tight and your shoulder tucked hard. You're too tense. I need you to loosen up a bit. Have a breather and have another go when you're ready.' The young man gave him a thumbs up and walked off towards the pens. Neville turned to Nick and Joanna. 'Now, I've got some things to do, feel free to look wherever you need.'

Joanna followed Nick down the steep steps of the gantry towards the bleachers. His eyes were on the cattle pens and the arena. 'What do you think?' she asked.

He shrugged. 'This whole blow up with Casey Blackwood and Neville Ford. I feel like this has something to do with it. And somehow, I still feel that Cameron Parsons has something to do with this.'

'I don't see it,' Joanna replied. 'Dean Taranto. I'd like to speak with him. Ask him what happened back then.'

'I think we do both. Let's have a quick look around here then I think we need to go and ask Casey Blackwood his side of the story. After that we'll look into Cameron's few weeks away. I just think with what they found in Matty's system, it ties to this somehow. There's a thread there, some sort of connection that I want to try and make.'

***

They made their way out the other side of town back towards Moroco. Joanna looked out the window as Nick drove and tried to piece together where they were at. She didn't know if they were close to a breakthrough or leading themselves up the garden path. Young Matty had been full of prescription drugs and now they had clear evidence that Casey Blackwood was selling those types of drugs. Even though it was years ago, it was an odd coincidence. Nick continued on past Moroco and turned down the driveway on the highway and drove past the sign 'Riverleigh'.

'John Blackwood bought this place ten years ago. Casey lives here with his wife and kid. When they bought it, it made Moroco one of the biggest farms in the region,' she said.

Nick looked through the windscreen and said nothing, seemingly deep in thought. He slowed as they reached the house and they both looked at it in wonder. The homestead for Riverleigh was enormous. Twice the size of the home at Moroco. It was double storey and red brick with a wraparound veranda on the top floor with the intricate Federation-style trimmings and fretwork of a home from the era. Everything about the property screamed opulence. Joanna spotted a white Range Rover Sport next to a Toyota Landcruiser ute, and behind the home she could see horse stables.

Nick whistled. 'And people say farmers have no money?'

They both climbed out of the car and walked to the front door, still eyeing the impressive façade. Joanna walked up the polished hardwood steps onto the porch. The decking here had been laid with an intricate herringbone pattern. She'd never seen anything like it. She walked up to the door and knocked. Nick pointed to a camera beside the door and a doorbell.

'Hello?' came a voice through the speaker.

'Hi, we were hoping Casey was home? We wanted to speak with him.'

There was silence at the end of the line and then a reply, 'Give me a minute.'

The sound of footsteps on a wood floor grew louder and a woman opened the door. She was tall and blonde and had the figure of a runner. She was tanned and looked like she took care of herself. She wore cream coloured horse-riding pants and Joanna could see the Ralph Lauren logo on her dress shirt. The woman smiled warmly at both of them, her teeth were perfectly straight and a brilliant white. 'Hi detectives, come inside please. He's out back.'

Joanna raised her eyebrows at Nick and he held a pinkie finger up as though he was having a cup of tea: the universal sign of class and wealth. She stifled a chuckle; he hadn't lost his sense of humour. She followed the woman inside and wasn't surprised to see the state of the inside matched the outside. Polished hardwood floors lined the long hallway, the walls were painted sage green, and ancient black and white images of farming activities plastered the walls. The property, over 100 years old, still had the smell of a new home build.

The woman stopped abruptly. 'Sorry, I'm Tori by the way. Casey's wife. He's told me all about you both. He says you are going to help us find Matty's killer?'

'We hope to,' Joanna replied. 'Your home is beautiful.'

'Thank you. We've just finished a fairly substantial renovation.'

They continued on past various bedrooms and into the lounge and dining area. There was a young toddler whose face was a metre away from the TV watching The Wiggles. 'Hot Potato' was in full force and she was jumping up and down and dancing to the beat. 'You look like you've got your hands full,' Joanna said.

Tori laughed. 'You don't know the half of it.' She pointed towards a second hallway that ran off a state-of-the-art kitchen. 'He's in his office, second door to the left.'

Chapter Thirty-One

Nick knocked lightly on the office door and heard Casey say, 'Come in.'

The office was big. There was a bookshelf on one side filled with leatherbound books. A ceiling fan above them circled and Casey's desk sat in the centre of the room, framed by two floor-to-ceiling windows. Nick's mind for some reason transported him back to Warranilla, and the office of Russell Waterford.

Casey Blackwood stood up. 'Detectives, how can I help you both today? Please take a seat.'

Nick looked at his desk. It was the polar opposite of Archie the Inspector's. The keyboard was perfectly symmetrical with the edge of the desk. Papers were lined up in a similar fashion, even the two pens beside it were in perfect symmetry. Nick was struggling to get a proper read on Casey Blackwood. He had his first impression: it was one of a man who was heir to one of the biggest properties in the state, a hard worker and a family man.

And then he had the story from Neville Ford, of a younger man who seemed tied up in some serious illegal activity.

'Your home is beautiful,' Joanna said again.

Casey smiled. 'Thank you.' He sighed. 'When the old owners moved out of it, it was near derelict. Shitload of work has gone into getting it to look like this.'

'And a shitload of money by the looks,' Nick added.

Casey laughed. 'Yeah, that too. The farm's been good to us.'

'Not for everyone though,' Nick said. Half of the state had been going through a record drought. And this region had been no different. He'd seen failed crops all over on this drive towards Gabinda. 'Drought's everywhere at the moment. You have to be able to afford the water.' Nick knew the government allocated water to the farmers for their crops. And with how bad the drought currently was, a lot of farmers were having to sell their water rights away. 'Looks like you've bought up some rights to keep the Moroco crop from spoiling.'

'You know your farming,' Casey said. 'Dad said you're from Milford. Nice little spot.'

'Paradise,' Nick replied.

'Is this about Matty?' Casey asked. 'Have you guys had any luck yet?'

'Yes and no,' Nick said. He knew whatever he would say would get back to the whole Blackwood family, and he wasn't sure where his gut instinct was leading him. But he wanted to be 100 percent sure before he made too many assumptions.

'We wanted to talk about the past a little bit if we could,' Joanna said. 'Specifically the falling out you had with Neville Ford. And the falling out Neville and your father had.'

Casey placed his hands on top of his head and leaned back in his chair. 'Why? What's this got to do with Matty? You reckon Neville Ford's got something to do with this?'

'We aren't ruling anything out, Casey. Just following up on a couple of different enquiries for now. We just wanted to hear the story from your side.'

'It's ancient history anyway, but alright then. When I finished private school, I was a bit of a lost cause. Bounced between Sydney and Gabinda a fair bit. I had a degree but didn't know what to do with it. I ended up hanging around the Ford property a bit. I wanted to be a bull rider.' It wasn't the story Neville had put forward, Nick thought, but he let him continue. 'Neville was always kind to me. I became mates with a few of the blokes back then. That's how I first met Cameron. Before him and Gabby shacked up together.'

'So, what happened? How did the disagreement start?'

Casey shrugged. 'I was young, I was a bit stupid. Takin' risks, ya know? I used to deal a little bit of pot.' He looked up at them. 'Nothin' huge, not commercial quantities or anything. But Nev caught me back in the day. I was trying to sell a bit to a few of the guys.'

'Just pot?' Joanna asked.

'Yeah. Anyway, Neville blew up. Screamed in my face. I thought he was gonna flog me. I'd never seen him that mad. He's right against drugs. Can't stand them. I get it now, but back then was different, I was a dumb kid. I made a mistake. After that I never sold or went near the shit again. I thought my old man was going to kill me.'

'Who were you trying to sell to?'

Casey looked down at his hands for a moment, lost in thought. 'Cameron definitely. And the other bloke's name was Dean, I think? He's been with Nev forever; still see him around a bit.'

'So you weren't selling Oxycodone or any other pills like that?'

Casey laughed. 'Far out, no way. I know how dangerous all that stuff is.'

'Okay,' Nick replied. It was an interesting story, and one he wasn't sure he believed. He stood up to shake Casey's hand. 'Thanks for the chat, Casey. That's all we need for now.'

Casey seemed confused. 'That's it? What's that got to do with my nephew going missing? I've got nothing to do with this, Detective.' He looked at Joanna. 'I spent the whole night searching for him. You saw me there.'

'I did,' Joanna replied. 'You currently aren't a person of interest, Casey. This is just a formality.'

That seemed to calm him a bit and he dropped back down into his chair. 'Fair enough. If you need absolutely anything from me or Dad, please let me know. He's not the most approachable of blokes sometimes but I'm always happy to help.'

'Will do,' Nick replied as they walked out of the office.

Nick drove away from the conversation at Riverleigh full of doubts. He'd seen many young men do stupid things and turn their life around, and Casey Blackwood seemed to be no exception. They'd looked up his record and found zero convictions, which seemed to further fortify his image as an upstanding member of the community. But something in his gut told him different. He couldn't place his finger on it. He didn't know whether it was just the bruised face of Cameron, or the tox report that Troy read out to them and the similar names of the illegal painkillers that filled Casey's nephew's system. He tried to sort through everything in his head, but by this time of the day, once again it had begun to ache. The headache would start behind his left eye, and gradually get bigger and bigger until his whole head ached. As he drove, he lightly touched his left eye with his thumb and winced, even the smallest fraction of pressure on his eye socket seemed to ease the pain ever so slightly.

'You okay?' Joanna asked.

'I don't know,' Nick said. It was the truth, he didn't know. He'd never worried about his own health before. He was your typical country bloke. If it bled, you chucked some tape over it. If it ached, you didn't talk about it. And if you caught feelings about anything, no-one was ever to know. But this was a totally different beast. This was his brain. And for the first time ever, he felt scared. Now, he knew he would never admit that to Joanna, but he could tell she saw his concern.

'If you need to take a break, I've got this Nick. I can do this. I know I can.'

He could see the steely determination in her eyes. He didn't doubt she could do it. He just had to prove to himself that he was still capable of being the detective he'd always been. 'I know you can, Joanna. I don't doubt you for a second. We both need answers on this for different reasons. I need to know whether I'm still capable of doing this.'

Joanna laughed. 'You're doing it right now, Nick.'

Nick's phone rang and he answered it quickly, he was feeling uncomfortable being so vulnerable around his partner. 'Detective Sergeant Vada speaking.'

'Nick, it's Troy. Just a small update. We've managed to get a full DNA sample from underneath the fingernails. I've sent it off for a database check, so fingers crossed something might pop up.'

'Good work. Thanks.'

He hung up the phone and turned the stereo up. It had been a long day, and he didn't know why it hit him at that very moment. The taste buds right on the end of his tongue seemed to activate all at once; he needed a beer.

'Shall we call it for the day?' he asked Joanna. 'Pub again?'

Joanna locked her iPad and placed it down in the footwell of the car. 'Don't have to ask me twice.'

Chapter Thirty-Two

Glenn balanced on the top edge of the gate and kept his boot locked in the gap between the two panels on the arena side. The bull in front of him smashed the cage with its horns, loudly protesting its captivity while a young rider hovered above it preparing to drop down into the chute and start his run.

He was in Condobolin and wasn't overly enthusiastic about wasting his energy on this Thursday night run. The crowd was paltry, locals who had bought a two-night pass for the rodeo had been invited in for the so-called training session, watched and applauded now and then, but he knew he was better than this. He wondered how he had got here. He had ridden in some of the biggest events in the world and now he was riding shows in front of a handful of people; it wasn't where he wanted to be. He wished he could turn back time, back to the one moment that had changed his life forever: It was in Texas, when he had been given his first ever ride in the Pro Bull Riding Tour where he had smashed his shoulder almost beyond repair on the first night, and since then luck had just never seemed to be on his side.

He had done all the right things back then. He had listened to his physical therapist, had done all the exercises, everything required to get his shoulder back to where it was strong enough to ride again, but the reconstruction was not fully successful. The surgeon, in his opinion, hadn't done the best job and he had been able to tell from the minute his doctor told him he could ride again that he was never going to be the same. He could handle the looseness in the joint, and the occasional re-dislocations, but what he couldn't handle was the pain. He wasn't even thirty back then but was living with daily pain, the dull, throbbing, aching waves that never seemed to go away. He hadn't known if he had it in him to live with it for much longer, it was that bad.

It all changed when he had met Dean. Dean was an old family friend and had ridden with his father for the one summer when his dad had wanted to be a bull rider. Dean was a man of few words but when he did speak he would give valuable insight, and Glenn knew to keep close and learn as much as he possibly could from the veteran rider. The biggest thing however, the thing that bonded the two men was their pain. One night by a campfire Dean had laid it all out to him over a beer. He had a horrific back injury back in his twenties and had sections of his spine fused. Like Glenn, the surgery never took and he had lived with excruciating pain over the last twenty years. But for him it was different, he had found a way to ease that pain through prescription pain medication. He had told Glenn about all of the types, oxycodone, fentanyl, and morphine, to name a few. He had passed a single tablet to Glenn in the darkness. He still remembered the colour, the blue of the tablet in the flickering flame. Dean had told him to take it easy, take half now and half at lunchtime the next day and report back, and tell him how he felt.

How he had felt had been easy to describe. Incredible. The dull throbbing aches when he would lie down had disappeared during the night. The months of tossing and turning and terrible sleeps had disappeared and were replaced with complete relaxation. He still remembered the next morning, when he had found Dean and told him excitedly what it had done for him. Dean had been happy for him but told him he needed to be careful. What he had given him was an incredibly powerful painkiller, and he needed to watch his intake as it could get extremely addictive.

His shoulder slowly got better over the last three years. He had continued his rehab, and with the help of the painkillers that he had been buying regularly from Dean he felt that he had control of his life again. He had no idea where Dean got the tablets from but chose to not ask. He didn't want to know.

Dean was selling small amounts to other riders that he knew, but he never advertised it. Glenn remembered a year ago when he had met Benji, and Benji had mentioned his sister was a cop, Dean had given him a knowing look over his beer glass: Benji could never be one of us. He never wanted his supply to end so knew to keep his mouth shut.

The last few months though, he had begun to notice a change in his friend. The strong and confident Dean was changing, into an angrier, meaner and more bitter man. He tried to figure out the exact moment it had happened but couldn't put a finger on it. He felt like any chance that it could, life would knock Dean down.

A year back, Dean had come off a bull during a training session in the Ford's arena. Glenn still had the image of the fall etched in his mind. Dean was launched backward off the bull and had come down directly on his backside. They all heard the crack of his tailbone as it smashed into the hard, red dirt and he had been one of the first people on the scene. Wendy had to call an ambulance, which was rare at the Ford farm. He'd spent a week in emergency while they tried to assess whether the fused section of his back had been affected, and to allow the chip in his tailbone to heal.

Dean's usual cheery demeanour never seemed the same after that injury, and Glenn wondered whether the doctors may have told him he needed to stop riding. That would have been a death blow for him, Glenn knew that; bull riding was Dean's life, and his one and only source of income. The sponsors had dried up and now he was only living off prize money, he had told him that. If he couldn't ride it would be back to the life of farming, which to Glenn, didn't sound that bad.

The training session ended and Glenn hadn't bothered riding. They returned back to their camp and sat around the fire. He watched Dean closely, he hadn't ridden either and as his beer bottle rested on his knee in the camping chair, it shook ever so slightly. 'Why didn't you ride today?' Glenn asked.

Dean sipped his beer by the campfire. 'Because I'm older and wiser than the lot of you. I'm not hurting myself again for nothing.'

'Only one way to get better.'

Dean scoffed. 'Didn't see you out there.'

Dean was right. Glenn knew that, and it was a touchy subject, frankly, he wasn't sure if his heart was still in bull riding. After what had happened to Bryce in Gabinda, he was starting to finally have second thoughts. His shoulder had gotten stronger over the last year, but he didn't know whether he still had what it took to face the bright lights. To sit on that fifteen-hundred-pound beast and risk your life. For what? Ten grand? Had it ever been worth it? he wondered.

'I know,' Glenn sighed, he was thankful the other riders had gone into town to the pub. He wouldn't have had this conversation with anyone else. 'I just don't know if I've still got it in me.'

Dean looked up from his beer. 'I'll be honest, Glenn, I don't think I do either.' His eyes were clear and his expression was stern. 'Why don't we just get the hell away from here? I've got a mate over west with a big property. Go work over there. Hell, we could even work in the mines.'

Glenn looked at his old friend. It was an odd comment to make. He had spent the last fifteen years on and off the Ford farm. Why did he all of a sudden want to leave it?

Chapter Thirty-Three

The pub was a lot quieter than it had been the night before and Nick stood at the bar waiting for the bartender who was taking a dinner order. She looked like she was young enough to still be in high school and when she walked over, he noticed she had braces. 'Hello,' she said.

'G'day.' Nick looked at the taps. Joanna wanted a white wine and he had tossed up for the last hour on what to do. If he had a beer he'd just get a light or a mid-strength, nothing too hard on his body. His mouth salivated at the thought. 'Ahhh, just a white wine. Sav blanc. And I'll get, ahhh, a Great Northern please.'

'No worries.' The girl walked to the fridges and grabbed two glasses. She poured Joanna's wine and then made her way back and poured his beer. As she was pouring it, she spoke. 'I'm a big fan, you know.'

'You are?' he asked.

She smiled again. 'Yeah. I listened to the podcast 'Into the Flames' like three times. I did my year end essay in Year 12 on it.'

'Oh yeah? How'd you go?'

'A+, of course. I still can't believe you solved it. Over twenty years, that poor family had no answers and you came in and solved it.' She snapped her fingers. 'Just like that.'

'It wasn't that easy, you know,' Nick replied, thinking back to his time back in Darfield and that case. He was nowhere until all of a sudden he got a break. Most cases were like that. The eventual buildup of evidence could only get you so far, and sometimes you needed good fortune as well. 'I was lucky.'

She held up a glass of water in his direction. 'Well, cheers to that. This town believes in you. Half the people in here are saying you'll find who killed the young Blackwood.'

He walked away, not feeling overly enthusiastic after the pep talk. Joanna was chatting to another waitress, a young girl he had seen a few nights back, and he sat down and slid the drink over to her.

'Thanks,' she said. She held her glass up in his direction towards the beer. 'Back on the horse?' She seemed tentative as she asked. 'Is, is that okay with the doctors? Have you asked them?'

'Yes, it's okay,' he replied. He wasn't actually sure but didn't care at that moment. He tipped the beer down and felt it cool his insides. The alcohol made his head buzz, in a good way. 'Ahhh. God, that's good.'

Joanna looked at him warily. 'Let's just take it slow, yeah?'

Nick laughed. 'I'm a big boy. I can handle myself.'

Dinner came and they both tucked into a beautiful meal, Nick was adamant that he still thought Cameron Parsons had something to do with it but Joanna was not so sure. He held his fifth beer up to his mouth and could feel his head spinning as the alcohol was hitting his bloodstream, he decided there and then that this would be his last beer for the night.

As he drank it, something behind Joanna's head caught his eye. He could just make out two men under the streetlamp in the car park. They were jammed between two cars but seemed to be in a heated discussion. He pointed over Joanna's shoulder. 'Check it out.'

Joanna turned around and they both watched on. They could hear raised voices and Nick quickly realised the men were about to fight. One of the men was taller than the other and stepped backwards further into the light as his arm went back to swing. The taller man hit the smaller man in the face, and the man crumpled and fell down between the two cars. It wasn't the fight that had interested Nick; it was what he had seen in that split second under the streetlights: the tribal neck tattoo of Cameron Parsons.

'Oi!' Nick yelled out as Cameron ran off into the night.

Nick jumped out of his chair and vaulted over the handrailing of the deck. He heard Joanna's seat crash onto the ground and could hear her close behind him as he ran out into the car park. He pointed to the figure between the cars. 'You check on him. I'm going after Cameron,' Nick yelled.

The only lights in the quiet residential street were the sparsely set streetlamps, Nick burst out onto the quiet road and spotted Cameron's tall figure under the next streetlight along, about fifty metres away. Nick sprinted along the footpath and shouted for Cameron to stop, but it was no use. As Cameron hit the third streetlight, Nick had closed the gap in half and as Cameron hit the corner, he turned to see who was chasing him. Nick saw the whites in Cameron's eyes, in shock at how he was so close, and Cameron spun and ran into the darkness down the driveway of one of the homes. Nick sucked in air as hard as he could, unable to believe how much of his fitness he had lost after his accident.

He sprinted down the dirt driveway and heard an aggressive dog barking.

'Oi, Dusty! Shut up!' A light had come on and a man had popped his head out of the side security door. When he saw Nick, he stopped. 'Who the hell are you?'

Nick quickly pulled out his badge; he didn't feel like being shot for trespassing. 'Police. Go back inside.' The man closed the door slowly again and Nick had a thought as he stopped. 'Hey Mister. Is the dog chained up?'

'Yep. In his kennel in the back corner.'

Nick gave him a thumbs up. He at least had that information to himself. Cameron had run down there clueless. There was a carport at the end of the driveway with two cars in it. The sides were open but the back wall was closed in. The dog continued to bark, a deep aggressive bark and Nick imagined whatever type of dog that Dusty was, he wasn't happy people were in his space. There was a chain link fence that went down the side of the carport that enclosed the yard. He hadn't seen where Cameron had gone, but he stopped at the opening of the carport and made an educated guess.

'If you're in here Cameron, stand up now. Don't try and get away or that dog's going to get you. If you give it up now, I'll go easy on you, mate. I know you've been through a lot over the last few weeks. Just talk to me.'

Nick's senses were on high alert. The homeowner yelled out again from behind him over the dogs loud barks. 'Dusty! Shut it!' and suddenly he was back in near silence again. He waited another five seconds and then heard a noise coming from the front of one of the cars. Cameron Parsons stood up slowly with hands up and a sheepish look on his face and walked in Nick's direction.

'I can explain,' he said.

Nick looked at the purple bruising on his face and tape over the cut in his lip. He wondered what the hell he was doing in the pub car park fighting at this time of the night when his partner was at home grieving. 'You can,' Nick replied. 'Back at the station.'

Nick marched Cameron all the way back to the car park and put him in the back seat of his car before checking on the man who had been punched.

'Gary Thommers. Thirty-three years old.' Joanna read from his licence. 'Lives in Gabinda.'

The man was leaning against a car beside them, nursing his jaw. He was scrawny and had a terrible tattoo of Ned Kelly on his arm. 'What happened here?' Nick asked.

Joanna handed him a packet of pills. 'Oxy,' she said.

'This yours?'

The man grimaced. 'Yeah. But I can explain.'

'Explain,' Nick said.

The young man looked over his shoulder. 'It's for my dad. He's got pancreatic cancer. Late stage. He's only got a few months left to go. Hospital never gives us enough for the pain. I just want to help ease his suffering.'

A likely story, Nick thought. And sounded well-rehearsed. 'Where is your dad now?'

Gary's mouth opened as if he were about to speak and then he stopped. 'He's, ah, at home.'

Nick didn't have time for this. 'Why did Cameron punch you?'

Gary shrugged. 'I owe him money.'

'How much?' Joanna asked.

'$500.'

'That's a lot of pills,' Nick said. 'Your old man must be real sick.' He looked back at Cameron in the back seat of his car. He wanted to push Cameron for more information about the murder, and having this gave him leverage. 'You want to press charges?'

Gary shook his head. 'Nah. Don't want nothing to do with him.'

Nick pointed away from the pub. 'On your way then. Night.'

Chapter Thirty-Four

The station was manned only by the young Constable Webb, and his look was one of astonishment when Joanna and Nick marched Cameron into the interview room. Nick placed Cameron down on one side of the table and then went back out to speak to Joanna.

'I want to press him for answers on where he's been. I want to make him sweat. We're going to tell him Gary wants to press charges. If he doesn't give us any information, I'm going to tell him we'll arrest him.'

Joanna nodded. 'Good idea.'

Nick stepped into the interview room and sat down beside Joanna. He watched Cameron closely as he spoke. 'Detective Sergeant Nick Vada and Detective Joanna Gray. Interviewing Cameron Parsons after witnessing an assault in the carpark of the Gabinda Hotel.' Nick looked at his watch. 'At roughly 10 pm.'

Cameron's hands weren't cuffed and he rested them on the table with a resigned look on his face. Nick started with a soft ball. 'Cameron, you know why you're here?'

'Yep.'

'You mind telling me what you were doing in the carpark of the Gabinda Hotel? And why you punched Gary?'

'I had some old painkillers. Gary's a mate. His mum's sick. Leant him some.'

'His mum?' Joanna asked before looking at Nick with a sly smile. 'I thought he said it was his dad?'

'Mum, dad, whatever,' Cameron replied.

Nick held up Cameron's wallet. Joanna had fished it out of his side pocket while he was in the backseat. It was full of $50 notes. 'You look flush with cash. Where's it all from?'

'Working. Bit of this, bit of that.'

Nick was getting annoyed. Cameron wasn't co-operating. 'Cameron we are going to arrest you for assault if you don't start talking. You want us to call Gabby? Tell her where you are? Why have you got painkillers like that on you?'

Cameron stared back at him defiantly. 'Can if you want. I did nothing wrong.'

Nick pulled the packet of painkillers he'd taken off Gary in the car park, onto the table. He hated doing things like this, but he could play dirty. He read out the back of the packet. 'Oxycodone. Controlled release. 10mg.' He looked at Joanna who seemed unsure what he was up to. 'Pretty powerful stuff.' He turned back to Cameron. 'I know you helped pick up Matty yesterday. Bringing him home for the funeral and all that. What the coroner didn't tell you was that your son was drugged to the eyeballs when he died. Full. 100mg's of this shit,' he said pointing down at the table. 'We don't know if it was the drugs or the person who strangled him that killed him.'

Cameron's hands on the white table clenched and then unclenched. Nick could see the violent reaction his words had made on the man. His face slowly turned red and tears welled in his eyes. It was harsh, no-one deserved to hear about how their child had died, but he'd worked with many people like Cameron before. Cameron was crook, and he knew something, Nick knew he did, he just needed prompting to spill the information.

'With oxy?' Cameron asked.

Nick nodded. 'Oxy, fentanyl, and some traces of morphine. Same shit you're selling in this little town, Cameron. Can't you see how this is all a little bit of a coincidence?'

Cameron stood up suddenly. 'I didn't fucking do it! I had nothing to do with Matty! I'm telling you right now! You can test me for blood or DNA or whatever you lot are doing these days.'

Nick stood up to face him. 'We'll take you up on that, Cameron, but I want more. Where the hell have you been? Why does your face look like that?'

Cameron fell back down to the chair in defeat. He breathed in and out and wiped the tears from his eyes. 'It was Casey and John. They, they told me I needed to go away for a while.'

'Why would they say that?' Joanna asked.

Cameron shrugged. 'I don't know alright! John told me he thought I had something to do with it!' Cameron pointed to his eye. 'See this? Casey bloody belted me. Tried to get me to talk.'

Nick looked at Joanna, now they were getting somewhere. 'Why would they do that to their own family? What would make them think that you would do that to Matty?'

'I don't fuckin' know!' Cameron yelled.

Joanna changed tack. 'Cameron, we need real information here. Your boy was loaded with drugs. Drugs we've now proven that you sell. Who are you getting them from? Is Casey Blackwood still involved? We need to know his involvement.'

Cameron shook his head. 'Casey's not involved. I bloody know it. He had nothing to do with this, I swear. He wouldn't hurt my boy.'

'We need to know where the drugs come from,' Nick said.

Cameron shook his head. 'I can't help you. I'm sorry. The stuff I gave to Gary is old stuff I had left over, got it from Dean back in the day.'

'Dean Taranto?' Joanna asked.

'Yeah. Rides out for Neville Ford. He's got a dodgy back. He's always had a good supply.' Cameron stopped. 'You don't think he's involved do you?'

Nick wasn't buying it. He wasn't sure that Dean had anything to do with it, otherwise why would he have helped Joanna and Amelia look for Matty's mobile phone? 'I think there is more to this story,' Nick said, 'I think you're not telling us what you know.' He stood up. 'I'm putting you in the lockup for the night, while we decide on your charges.'

'Can I at least call Gabby?' Cameron asked. 'Let her know where I am.'

'We'll do that,' Joanna replied.

Nick led him into the single lockup cell and switched the light on. He had to suppress a smile. The cell was tiny, with only a concrete bench that acted as a seat and bed, and a dirty old toilet bowl. It was a forgotten memory of the cells of yesteryear. He was almost pleased it hadn't been updated. He wanted Cameron Parsons to sweat overnight. If he had something to say, he'd be saying it by the morning.

They walked down the hallway back into the offices. Constable Webb sat his desk and sipped from his coffee. 'What do you want me to do with him?'

Nick smiled. 'Nothing. Leave him for tonight. We'll be back tomorrow to speak with him again.' He looked at his watch, it was already 11 pm. 'C'mon Jo, let's try and get a bit of rest before tomorrow. Big day.'

Chapter Thirty-Five

Benji woke up early. The unfiltered rays of sunlight beamed directly across his face from the double-hung window in the bedroom of the old house. The curtains looked like they were about fifty years old, and he rolled over and tried to flick them across to shade his eyes from the intense light.

He stared up at the water stain on the ceiling. He had been excited about the prospect of staying at Dean's place while he was away, but now, after sleeping here for three nights, he was starting to miss the modern bunkhouse and the crew of riders that were up there. He rolled out of bed gingerly, and stood up slowly, yawning and stretching his arms above his head. He'd come off in the shed the day before and looked at himself in the mirror. A big angry purple bruise had spread itself across his left arm and down his side, it was a stinger, and a good one. He was going to be feeling it for a week or two, that was for sure.

He walked into the lounge room of the house and on through to the kitchen. He placed two pieces of bread in the toaster and searched through Dean's cupboard. *Jackpot*, he thought as he pulled out a new jar of Vegemite. He poured himself a cup of tea, buttered up his toast nice and thick and put only the lightest of spreads across his toast. He thought back to his childhood with Joanna. She used to spread her Vegemite on thick and he was the total opposite. She had always had a go at him over it.

The front deck on the house was old, there were gaps between the decking boards where people in the past had stepped through and snapped the distressed pieces of timber, and the green plastic chairs against the front wall had seen better days. He carefully carried his hot tea out with his toast and took a seat. It was peaceful being there all alone. As dingy a place as Dean's was, it was nice to finally have a place of his own for the time being. His thoughts once again drifted to his sister. He thought about her out at the farm yesterday with her partner, Nick. It was nice having her around. He felt proud seeing what she had become, after the way their father had treated them. Joanna had received the brunt of it. The physical abuse came in fits and spurts, less and less as they got older, because their father was so drunk half the time he couldn't stand up. The verbal abuse took a worse toll though. Their father was the most negative man put on this earth, and Benji smiled at the positivity that seemed to shine from his sister. It was like a lifelong protest against the way her father had treated her. He respected that.

After his fall, Neville had pulled him into his office and told him he was giving him a week off. He was pushing the training too hard and he needed a break, Neville said. He didn't deserve the leniency, he thought, but he knew Neville must see something in his riding that he didn't quite yet. He wanted to show Neville, prove to him that he could be the best rider he could be, so he graciously accepted the offer to work on the farm for a week and let his arm and side heal up.

After breakfast, he showered and put on some old clothes. As he walked towards his ute, his phone rang. Dean was calling from Condobolin and he was excited to hear an update of how the blokes went on training night. 'Morning.'

'Morning yourself. How's the place going?' Dean said, he sounded like he was in a good mood.

'Place is good. Needs a good tidy up. I'm not your missus though. I'm just sleeping there and working. You can do that when you're back.'

Dean chuckled. 'Fair enough.'

'You sound like you're in a good mood. You ride well yesterday?'

'No. I didn't ride actually. Either did Glenn. We just spectated. I'm not breaking myself with no crowd there to watch.'

Benji was confused. Neville had strict rules around training. You didn't train, you didn't ride the big show. 'I thought Neville said you have to train or you won't ride the show?'

'What Nev don't know, won't hurt him, Benji.'

'Fair enough. Not my place to say anything.'

Benji could hear Dean speaking to someone in the background. 'Heard you come off the other day? Took a big hit? This one of your firsts?'

The comment made his side throb, he'd forgotten it for a short moment there. 'Yeah. Landed right on my side. Nev's got me off for the next week. Going to help him out around the farm.'

'Yeah, I heard. What's he got you doing? He was talking about drenching those sheep the other week.'

Benji couldn't think of anything worse at that moment, chasing and herding sheep around a paddock would've been terrible for his shoulder. 'Nah, you know the green stock crate that's next to the machinery shed? He wants me to clean it out. I think he's lending it to the Kesslers for their next stock sale.'

There was silence for a moment. 'The green one beside the house? Didn't Mack Morton pick that up last night? He was borrowing it for the rodeo?'

'Nah. Neville said he changed his mind. I'm not fussed. Gives me something to—'

Dean cut him off. 'I already cleaned it. I cleaned it last week after the rodeo, so you don't need to stress.'

'You did?' Benji was relieved. 'Shit, well you saved me a crappy job. I'll spend my time cleaning out the machinery shed then. Thanks, mate.'

'No worries,' Dean replied. 'When are you heading here? Is the whole crew coming? Neville and all?'

'Tomorrow. We're all heading up. Yep.'

'Good. Good to know. Look Benj, I got to go. I'll see you tomorrow alright?'

Benji hung up the phone and stood still next to his ute. The phone call was no different to the hundreds he'd had with Dean before, but something for some reason seemed off. He looked across towards the machinery shed and at the green stock crate. It was a trailer built by Cannon. Adorned on the side of it was their famous 'Beef Bus' stickers. Painted in blue paint across the top of the crate was 'FORD TRANSPORT', and he wondered why Dean's demeanour had changed so much when cleaning it was brought up. Something felt wrong.

Benji placed his phone and keys on the bonnet of his ute and walked to the trailer. Although Dean had said he'd cleaned it, the rear wheels were black with road grime and he could see the cow manure on the floor base. Dean had either lied or done a terrible job, he thought and he didn't want Neville to think he was slacking off so he decided to clean it anyway.

He unlatched the sliding bar that held the back ramp in place and lowered it to the ground then walked to the side wall of the machinery shed where the pressure washer was. Although he didn't really feel like cleaning out the trailer and being covered in cow shit, he knew the temperature was going to be pushing nearly forty today, and it was either this or cleaning out the stuffy machinery shed. He fired up the pressure washer and attached the detergent wand to the side of it. He checked the canister was full and then threw on a pair of gumboots and a rubber apron that hung on the hook next to it. He knew from previous experience that it was always best to drag the hose right up to the nose of the trailer and let the fall of the floor do its work, the heavy pressure from the hose would cause all of the muck to run out the back. 'Shit really does run downhill,' he said to himself as he dragged the heavy spray wand up the ramp.

Dean had lied, the inside of the trailer hadn't been cleaned, and the cow manure in it was thick and baked in hard from the weeks of heat. The smell had even gone away as the manure was so stale. Stepping across it, he realised he was going to have to try and get a shovel and scrape some of it out first. The water wasn't going to get it up.

He reached halfway and stopped. It was darker towards the nose of the trailer, but sunlight still beamed through the narrow gaps from each side, illuminating the scene in front of him. There was a red milk crate jammed in the corner, along with a bucket. He stepped up closer to inspect. There were two bottles of water and some muesli bar wrappers beside the milk crate. Benji was confused. He bent down to pick up the wrapper to inspect it. Had someone been sleeping in here, he wondered. It wouldn't be a nice place to stay.

As he dropped the muesli wrapper and looked at the metal slats that formed the side wall, he froze in shock. He dropped the metal pressure washer wand with a clang and immediately dropped to his knees down in the cow manure. He leaned in closer to see the word scratched into the green paintwork. His eyes were registering what he was seeing but his brain hadn't quite caught up from the shock.

It was one word. A name. Scratched into the paintwork. 'Matty.'

Chapter Thirty-Six

Nick quickly closed the main door of the men's bathroom in the police station, locked it and bent over the toilet bowl. He vomited hard; the type that burnt the back of your throat and gave you a headache from how hard you had to push.

When he was finished, he stood up and gripped the hand basin beside the toilet and looked in the mirror. He was a mess. For some reason, one eye was bloodshot and the other clear. His face was red and the yellowed dregs of vomit dripped down the stubble on his chin. I *need to clean myself up and sort myself out*, he thought. He wiped his face with a paper towel and ran his hands through his hair. He splashed a small amount of water on his face to try and wake up and reset himself. He was stupid; he shouldn't have mixed beer with the strong medicine he was on. He had taken an extra dose of his medication when he left this morning, hoping it would clear his head for what looked to be another long day.

He had spent the morning explaining to Archie and Amelia what had happened the night before. He watched them closely. What he and Joanna had done was not anywhere near usual police procedure, especially when the man Cameron had assaulted didn't want to press any charges, but he neglected to mention those few details, and the others didn't seem bothered by any of his techniques and his late-night interview. They seemed just as interested in finding justice for Matty as he was.

'So, what are you going to do?' Amelia asked.

'We'll let him go with a warning. No reason to hold him any longer for now. He'll be hurting after the things I said to him. I want to watch him though, I still have a feeling he's involved somehow.'

Amelia turned to Archie. 'And I want to know where he's getting that type of prescription medication. He's not getting it from the doctor's, that's for sure. If he's selling that type of stuff around town, he needs to go down for it.'

'What about Gabby? Could he be getting it from her?' Archie asked.

It was a point Nick had never thought of, and the first smart thing the Inspector had ever said, he made a mental note to ask her some more questions about that.

'Gary Thommers is a drop kick,' Archie added. 'His story about his sick mum or dad is bullshit. He's not from here, we've had him in here before.'

The door next to the reception slammed open and Nick spun around to see Joanna running towards the Inspector's office. She looked excited as she walked in.

'What's up?' Nick asked.

'I think we finally got our break.'

***

Nick and Joanna sped to the Ford farm with Amelia and other members of the Gabinda police in tow. As Nick drove, Joanna updated him on what Benji had said when he called her. 'Benji's out staying in the back house. Dean Taranto's. He's got a couple of old truck trailers near the machinery shed that Neville wanted him to clean out. He found some stuff in there. A milk crate, a bucket, some food scraps. He reckons Matty had been kept in there.'

It was all slowly coming together, it made sense now. 'Stock crates.' He hit the steering wheel. 'I should've thought of that earlier. That would explain the cow shit on Matty's shoes. He must have kept him in the stock crate.'

'Stock crate? They are the big cattle trailers?'

'Yep. Remember that big trailer at the arena you parked near? The one in your photos. Same thing.' Nick thought for a moment. 'So, it was out front of Dean Taranto's place?'

'Yes. He has to be involved.' She rubbed her hands down over her face. 'I hardly considered him. He just doesn't fit in any way. He was there that night with us. I can't believe it.'

'Let's just be sure before we make any rash calls,' Nick said. 'We could be wrong.'

Nick flew down the Ford's driveway with his lights flashing. He didn't stop at the Ford residence and watched in the rear view mirror as the giant dust cloud from his car and Amelia's four-wheel drive enveloped the home. If Dean Taranto had kidnapped and held Matty Blackwood they needed to secure the scene and investigate, and then they needed to find his location quickly. If Dean was tipped off in any way he could be gone in an instant.

They both pulled up at the ageing brick veneer home in a blinding cloud of dust. Nick got out and spied a white Landcruiser ute following in their direction then watched as Neville Ford and another cowboy got out and walked in his direction.

'What's this all about?' Neville asked Joanna.

'Benji called me,' Joanna said. 'He thinks he's found something in your green stock crate.'

'I know we should have stopped in at the house, but time was of the essence. Are we okay to search it, Neville?' Nick asked.

Neville looked onward to the crate. 'The crate? Sure.'

Nick and Joanna led the way with Neville and the rest of the Gabinda cops behind him. Benji stood over near the ramp and Nick ran his eyes over the trailer. It was a two-storey semi, painted a bright green with 'Ford Transport' painted at the front of it.

'Morning,' Benji said to the group.

'Thanks for the call, mate,' Nick said as he patted the man on the shoulder. 'It's tips like this that break this stuff wide open.' They all stood near the edge of the ramp. Nick was eager to take a look. 'So, what happened this morning?'

'I came out this morning and Nev asked me if I could clean out this trailer. It's getting picked up in a few days' time.'

'Kesslers are borrowing it for a stock sale,' Neville added. 'He's got a truck as well. Doesn't have a trailer big enough for what he needs.'

Benji continued, 'So, I was just about to get into it and Dean called me to say g'day. I mentioned in passing what I was doing and he acted a bit strange. He apparently thought it'd been picked up already?' Benji said looking over at Neville.

Neville nodded. 'Mack Morton was going to take it earlier on in the week. Ended up using one of his own.'

'Strange, you said?' Joanna asked.

'Yeah. After I told him it was still here and I was going to clean it, he cut me off, he said to not worry about it, it's already clean.' Benji pointed to the side of the trailer. 'That's when I walked over to check it out. It's not clean at all. It's filthy.'

'Anyone else been near this trailer in the last few weeks?' Nick asked Neville.

Neville shook his head. 'Nah. Any trailers down here don't get much use. All the good trailers are up near the arena. I don't come down here much at all myself, I haven't been here since before the Gabinda Rodeo. It's pretty much just Dean sticking to himself down here.'

Nick looked at Joanna. 'C'mon, let's take a look.'

Nick led the way and walked up the steep ramp of the cattle trailer. Being two-storey, he had to duck ever so slightly so his head didn't hit the floor beams of the second floor as he walked in. The base floor was a couple of inches thick with cow manure, and going by how firm it felt under his boot, it had been there for a while.

'Doesn't smell as bad as I thought it would,' Joanna said.

Nick chuckled. 'Try and come in one of these when they're fresh. It's not as pleasant.'

'It's down the far end,' Benji said from behind them.

Nick reached the nose of the trailer first. There was a milk crate, an old heavy-duty bucket and a few loose, empty water bottles. He bent down low and counted four muesli bar wrappers. It looked like someone had stayed in there.

'Look at this,' Joanna said, against the wall.

He knelt down as gently as he could, and together they looked at the name 'Matty' scratched into the dirt on the side wall of the trailer.

Joanna looked at him. 'He's held him in here. Like a hostage.'

'But why?' Nick asked.

'I don't know,' Joanna said. They were both stumped. Why keep the young boy here for weeks and then kill him?

'What did you touch?' Nick asked Benji.

'Nothing. One of the muesli bar wrappers.'

'We'll need to get your DNA and prints just to ensure you are cleared.'

'Of course.'

Nick grabbed one of the zip lock bags that was tucked into his back pocket. He pulled on a rubber glove and bagged each of the water bottles. 'We'll need to test these. Check if Matty's DNA is on them. We need to prove he was here.'

Neville joined them from behind and looked around, he bent down in the same spot Nick had and ran his hand over the scrawled name on the side of the trailer. He put his head into his hands. 'Jesus fucking Christ, Dean. Surely not.'

Joanna turned to Benji. 'Where is Dean right now?'

Benji rubbed his face, with a serious expression. He was clearly shaken, this Dean had been a close friend. He looked to be still trying to come to terms with the fact that his friend was possibly a murderer. 'He's in Condobolin with Glenn. The rodeo is tomorrow night.'

Nick walked out of the trailer and pulled the group of cops together. He turned to Archie. 'You need to control your local mob, not a word gets out to a soul. We can't have Dean Taranto hearing that we've found this. If he's done this, we need to catch up with him before he finds out what we know. We need the element of surprise.'

He walked over towards Neville and Benji, who were in an animated conversation. Neville looked shaken up at what he had seen, unable to comprehend the seriousness of what was happening. 'I know this is hard, but we need absolute confidentiality here. If Dean is really the only person who comes down here, he has to be the person who held Matty in here. He cannot know what we've found. If this is as serious as what it looks like, your friend could be a killer.'

Neville shook his head. 'I'm sorry, Detective, I just don't understand. Why the hell would he do this?'

'We still need to establish that. And I'm not going to single out the bloke until further testing has happened, but I need your word that no-one will tip him off.'

Both men nodded in agreement. Nick knew he was stuck between a rock and a hard place. He knew that people had their loyalties, but he had to trust them.

Chapter Thirty-Seven

Dean leaned against his ute and watched the sun rise. It was rodeo day and the shimmer of the days heat was always radiating across the horizon. As a younger man, he had loved the morning before the big show. He had fond memories of rolling out of his swag in the mornings with whatever beautiful young woman had fallen into it the night before, and sitting with them and watching the sun rise.

Those days of his youth were long gone and the repercussions of his younger and braver days had now caught up with him. He had fallen off during training a few months back. It hadn't been a bad fall, he'd had much worse, but as he sat in the emergency room with the doctor telling him he had a broken tail bone, and that he had re-injured a fused section of his spine, he realised he was never going to be able to ride competitively again.

The recovery had been worse than any one he'd ever been through before. Every inch, every cell in his body ached. All of his previous injuries seem to come back ten-fold like forgotten nightmares from the past. There were a few days where he holed up in his little house at the back of Neville's farm and didn't leave the bedroom because the pain was so bad. He simply didn't have the will to get up.

One thing had got him through those dark days. His pills. He had been taking strong pain medication for more than half his life now. Oxy was like Panadol to him, morphine gave him a little bit of relief but his main drug of choice these days was fentanyl. Cameron Parsons had sold him his first ever pill after one of his first big falls, and he had never looked back. Once they became friendly, Cameron had introduced him to a young Casey Blackwood and explained what Casey's arrangement was. Casey had said from the beginning that he was not a dealer, he was simply a storer, and that he never wanted to get involved with selling, it was simply too risky to the family name. But he and Cameron had always been allowed to sell a small quantity to make ends meet.

He had sold a little here and there over the years. If he'd had a bad season, the funds would more than help pick up the slack, but after this new injury, as he slowly recovered, he realised he was fast running through his savings. He had heard rumours about the Blackwood's operation and had finally found the big machinery shed near the national highway at the back of

Riverleigh after scoping out the properties. He did his research and hatched a plan with Cameron Parsons to break in and rob it. They had watched the place in the dead of night, watching the trucks coming in and out and how the deliveries were made. It was going to be their meal ticket. He learned there were hundreds of thousands of dollars' worth of pills in those pallets, and on one of the nights he was so close to the door he wanted to just sprint in and go for it, but Cameron was hesitant. He told him to wait.

Money kept getting tighter as he missed more and more rodeos, and he finally confronted Cameron. He was desperate, he needed money badly, he was in debt, and his usage after his back and tailbone injury had begun to worsen. His supply levels were dropping by the day. He had lost count of how many of the fentanyl tablets he had taken, and they were beginning to not work as well, so he was starting to apply patches on his chest and back. They were ingested through the skin and seemed to be doing the job for now, but he knew that you could build a tolerance to them. He needed more and he needed the money. Cameron had been firm. He'd changed his mind and said no, there was no way he was going to do it, something had seemed to scare him off.

There was no real grand plan, he'd never even thought of it until the night of the Gabinda Rodeo. He was desperate by then.

Neville had pulled him aside and asked him if he was going to ride and he'd been hesitant. Neville was firm, if he wasn't going to ride, they needed to sit down next week and hash out his next steps. He had been clear; if he didn't ride, he wasn't going to be welcome on the farm anymore, so he reluctantly geared up and hit a beautiful fifteen second, high scoring ride for his first run of the afternoon at the rodeo. He was surprised he had managed it, but adrenaline, and the four patches of Fentanyl had done enough to keep him upright. After the back patting, hand shaking and a nod of approval from Neville were given, he walked back to his ute, opened the back door and fell across the back seat. His body was shutting down, he couldn't do this anymore. His back and tailbone were on fire and he opened up his ute glovebox to see he was down to his last box of twenty patches. With the amount he was going through, he had built up a considerable debt with Cameron and Casey Blackwood, and it was one he was sure he'd never be able to repay.

He pulled another patch out of his pocket and placed the thin plastic under his tongue. Cameron had told him that if they had stopped working as well on the skin that he'd heard this was better. The relief was almost immediate and gave him enough strength to take off his gear, get changed into some fresh clothes as the sun set and go out for a walk around.

John Blackwood's daughter, Gabby, and Camerson Parsons were standing near the food area speaking with Benji and his sister Joanna, who he'd only just met. His eyes travelled across to their son, Matty. He'd never met the young boy, but he'd seen him on the odd occasion with his mum in town. Although Gabby Blackwood wasn't on speaking terms with her father, he'd heard that Matty still managed to spend time on the farm with his grandfather. That's when the idea hit him. It was like a bolt of lightning. The boy. He was John Blackwood's only grandson. The richest man in town. And a family with a secret worth blackmailing for. It would be simple. He would take Matty Blackwood. He had his pistol in his ute, if he could get Matty away from his parents, he would flash the pistol, take him to his ute and get the hell away before anyone noticed.

Once he had the boy, he knew that chaos would reign. He would do his best to help with the search, be the good friend to Cameron and help out where required. When the time was right, he would message John Blackwood and tell him he had him. Tell him he wanted a million dollars and the boy would be returned safely. Taking Matty had been easy and the next morning, while the young boy slept on the floor of the stock crate just outside his home, he typed the text message into the cheap plastic prepaid phone he'd bought at the petrol station.

Jason Summers

I HAVE THE BOY. 1 MILLION DOLLARS CASH DELIVERED TO ADDRESS I PROVIDE AND HE WILL BE RETURNED. IF MONEY IS NOT PAID I WILL KILL HIM.

Chapter Thirty-Eight

Joanna sat in the driver's seat of Nick's police vehicle. She was parked in the truck bay beside Lake Cargelligo. The water was a murky brown and dead calm. It was shaping up to be another scorching day and she got out and felt the searing morning sun beat down on her neck. She was full of indecision, she couldn't wrap her head around Dean Taranto being involved in the young boy's disappearance, she just didn't think that the quiet cowboy would have it in him, but she knew how desperate people could get and the lengths they were willing to go when money got tight. It was just taking time for her to comprehend it all.

She could see Nick down at the water's edge and she walked down the green grass towards him. His boots were on the bank with his socks rolled up inside them, and he was standing in the cool water with his pants rolled up with the water lapping just over his ankles. She had to smile. He was a river kid through and through; any brown murky water around and he was the first person who wanted to go jump in it. His right arm was waving animatedly as he spoke on the phone and he hung up and turned around when Joanna reached the edge.

'Couldn't help yourself, could you?' she asked.

He grinned. 'The water's like soup. I love it this time of year. I wish we had time for a swim.' He walked up the bank and sat down on the grass next to his boots. 'I've got news.'

'Yeah?'

'That was the Chief. The DNA results for the bottle were fast-tracked. I had told him it was a matter of urgency. He just got word back. DNA matches Matty Blackwood.'

'Far out,' Joanna replied. It was coming together much quicker than she had imagined. 'But the DNA on the bottle. That's not enough for a conviction?'

Nick shook his head. 'It's enough for us to bring him in on suspicion of murder. We can hold him for twenty-four hours. We'll get prints and DNA and check against the skin found under Matty's fingernails; I'm guessing that should be a hit. I've already requested his phone records so we can look through them, see if any tower pings line up with when Matty was taken.'

'Still no motive though,' Joanna said. 'I just don't understand why.'

The warm morning sun had done its job and Nick's feet dried quickly. He slipped each sock and then each boot on. He stood up and stretched, she could tell he was in a good mood. It was hard not to be. 'It's hard to know. But I think when we pull him in and lay all of this out, he'll either crumble and tell us everything or lawyer up. Either way we've got him where we want him.'

They grabbed food at the petrol station before the last leg of their journey. Joanna had told Nick about Glenn, after Benji had told her he was in Condobolin with Dean.

'Do you think I should text him? Feel him out?' Joanna asked.

'If you think he won't suspect anything, sure.'

'What do you think?'

Nick took a bite of the sandwich he held while he steered with his other hand. 'Worth a shot. As long as you don't think it'll scare him off?'

Joanna stared down at her phone screen. 'Nah, I think we go for it.'

She typed out a text message to Glenn. *Morning.*

Glenn replied quickly only a minute later. *Hey Jo, long time no speak. How's the case going?*

Slowly, but we are making small steps. Benji said you're at another rodeo?

Yeah. Condobolin, couple of hundred clicks away, so no chance of dinner unless you feel like driving haha.

Joanna sent a laughing emoji and then typed: *Are Bryce and Dean with you? I think Benji said he's heading over tomorrow?*

She waited as the text bar popped up and then went away. She wondered if she'd messed up, if she'd been too forthcoming. Surely Glenn wouldn't smell a rat?

Only Dean. Bryce is still at Nev's. Yep, Benji's riding. Could you get time off? You should come and watch the show. It might be my last.

That's an odd thing to write, she thought. Glenn had been one of the top-rated riders in Australia only a few years earlier, Benji had said, and he was still young. She wasn't sure why he would want to quit.

You giving up?

Yeah. Well, I don't know. I've been speaking with Dean a bit. He's thinking about quitting, moving away, you know?

Joanna looked up at Nick. The text thread had continued over the last hour and Nick said, 'We're ten ks out.'

'Good. He's just said Dean's quitting riding. Wants to move away.'

Nick smiled. 'That doesn't sound like an innocent man.'

***

The rodeo was a small affair. The stands around the makeshift arena were only three steps high and only half full of spectators. Some of the same food vendors from the Gabinda Show had made the journey over but the flashy Show rides hadn't followed. The rodeo in this town was a dying one, and as Dean balanced on top of the fence with his boots tucked under the railing, he wondered if they'd even have it the next year.

Glenn had suited up, he wore his black leather padded riding vest and black helmet. Dean was still old school. He was one of the last of the old crowd who still rode in his hat, for him there was a romanticism to it, the helmet seemed too new aged. He felt a bit like John Wayne and the famous cowboys of yesteryear when he launched out into the arena.

'You going to ride?' Glenn asked him.

Dean shook his head and waved his beer bottle in Glenn's direction. He was dangerously low now on his fentanyl patches and drinking was all he could do now to mask the pain. Cameron

Parsons had topped him up right before he'd gone walkabout, but now he was just about out and getting desperate again. He had kept a close eye on the police as much as he could during the investigation, even helping them find Matty's phone, but he still couldn't believe his body had surfaced in the Smith's dam. Hearing that the police had been out to the Ford farm, sniffing around and asking questions was when he realised that they were really circling. They were getting closer and closer to the truth and he didn't want to be a part of that. When Benji told him the day before that the Morton's hadn't taken the trailer he had kept Matty in, he became worried, but realised unless they really knew where to look, bulls would be loaded straight up the ramp any day now and the evidence of Matty's prison would be gone forever.

'You ever wonder if all this is worth it?' he asked Glenn, who watched the next rider come out of the chute.

'The riding? Sure.' Glenn laughed. 'When I was younger and my whole body didn't ache.'

'Not the riding. This life.' Dean replied, as he vacantly stared across the arena. 'The sacrifice. The hard work. For what?'

Glenn turned to him. 'You alright, mate?'

Dean sipped from the cold Corona he held in his hand, the alcohol mixing with the patches had slowed him down now, levelled him out. He was feeling introspective, and a little invincible. He looked out across the empty landscape and onward into the vast unknown. He could say goodbye to Glenn and be in another state in a few hours. Lost in the wind. And he would never need to worry about riding ever again. He could clean himself up. Get a real job. His brother was a bricklayer in the west, he could labour for him, get his life back on track. He wanted to forget the nightmare of the last two months all together.

Glenn turned away with a wide smile to speak to someone behind him. 'You couldn't stay away, could ya? G'day Nick, how are ya, mate?'

Dean froze. He knew who was standing behind him.

'Dean Taranto,' Joanna said.

Dean stepped down off the fence onto the hard red dirt. Half of the small crowd turned to see what was happening. The two Sydney detectives stood in front of him, both with grave expressions.

'Yeah?' he asked.

'Come with us, please. We'd like to speak with you in relation to the murder of Matty Blackwood.'

Chapter Thirty-Nine

Nick felt a little disappointed at the anticlimax. He didn't expect Dean Taranto to have come willingly, but the man simply smiled a sad smile and handed his beer bottle to Glenn, who was protesting on his behalf.

Dean had stayed silent in the back seat of Nick's car on the drive back to Gabinda, just looking out the window with his lips pressed firmly together. Joanna had tried to strike up conversation one time but he did not respond. Nick had given a small shake of his head when Joanna looked across at him. If the guy was guilty, he was stewing on it, deciding what his story was going to be. The shake of his head to Joanna simply said, give the man space, let him decide what he's going to do. By simply going with them and providing no resistance, he deserved a level of respect Nick never usually gave to potential child killers, but it seemed that the good manners of the bush still prevailed in some people.

Taking his fingerprints had been easy, and after that Joanna quickly took DNA swabs of the inside of his mouth and handed the samples to Amelia, who planned to rush them to the lab in Dubbo herself. It was the fastest way they could get them to Troy and get results back before their 24-hour window for keeping him would shut.

Nick walked him into the same interview room in which he'd spoken with Cameron Parsons and sat down across from him. He'd offered no resistance from the minute they'd grabbed him, and Nick decided to leave his cuffs off. He didn't come across to him as a flight risk.

'Detective Sergeant Nick Vada and Detective Joanna Gray commencing interview with suspect Dean Taranto. I'll start off with an easy question, Dean. Where are you currently residing?'

'The Ford farm. Neville gave me his back house to live in.'

'And what do you do on the farm?'

'I'm a bull rider. I ride for Neville's pro team. I'm currently ranked eleventh outright, for all men in Australia,' Dean said with pride.

'What else do you do on the farm?'

Dean shrugged. 'I help out when I'm injured. Which has been a lot more than usual the last two years. I'll drive a header during the harvest. I service machinery. Clean up a bit. Whatever Neville needs from me.'

'Ok, great.' Nick scrawled notes on his notepad. 'And did you attend the Gabinda Rodeo?'

'I did.' Dean pointed at Joanna. 'I met your partner Joanna there for the first time.'

'And did you see Matty Blackwood at the rodeo?'

Dean picked at his thumbnail and stayed silent. His face was slowly turning a shade of red. 'I did.'

Joanna leaned in and spoke. 'Did you take him Dean? We found the trailer. We know.'

Dean looked up in shock at Joanna. He gritted his teeth together and then rubbed his hand through his hair. 'The trailer. I didn't. I was. I didn't know.' He looked down at his feet. 'I didn't know what to do. I had him but I didn't know what to do.'

'You kept him in the trailer?' Nick asked. 'Why?'

Dean exploded. 'Because I needed the money! I was fuckin' desperate, alright? I'm a fuck up. My body is a wreck and I'm using worse than I ever have.' His eyes met Nick's. 'I had nowhere else to turn.'

Nick looked at the ageing cowboy with disgust. Any prior kindness he felt towards the man had dissipated. He was a killer and a drug addict. 'Using?' Nick asked.

'Fentanyl. Morphine. Oxy. Whatever I can get my hands on. I fucked my back a few years back, and now my tailbone's wrecked too. Never been the same since.'

'And that gives you an excuse to kill a child?' Joanna said.

'No,' Dean replied. 'I have no excuse for what I've done.'

'Tell us the whole story,' Nick said. 'From the start. The more you tell us now, the easier it will be. It will help with your sentencing as well when you are convicted.'

Dean sighed. 'Okay.' He fell silent and stared down into his hands for over a minute before he spoke again. 'I'm out of cash. Near broke. Neville spoke to me and told me if I didn't keep riding I'd be off the team. Any of the sponsors I had are long gone. I didn't know what else to do. I know the Blackwoods are loaded with all the operations they have going on and I knew how much John Blackwood loved that boy. I only decided the night I saw him talking to you, Joanna. It had worked out perfectly. I was hiding behind the stands watching the boy. He'd walked over to the food court as Bryce was injured. The whole town was looking one way, I went the other. I grabbed him. Put him in my ute and brought him out here. I locked him in the stock crate with a bottle of water and got back to the rodeo before anyone knew I was gone.'

No-one would've suspected a thing, Nick thought. Joanna had told him about Bryce's injury and the madness and confusion of Matty's disappearance. He could've easily slipped away and came back without being noticed.

Dean took a deep breath in and continued. 'I bought a prepaid phone. I sent a message to John Blackwood. I told him I wanted a million dollars or the boy would die.'

Nick turned to Joanna. They had spoken with the Blackwood's multiple times. How had John Blackwood not mentioned that? 'And did he reply?' Nick asked.

Dean threw his hands up. 'Not once. I didn't know what to do. A few weeks passed. I just kept giving him water and a bit of food. Some nights he cried out so loud I thought someone for sure would hear him.' Dean went quiet for a moment, clearly lost back in the young boy's moments of distress. 'Neville kept asking me about the trailer. I was paranoid, I thought he might know something. I was afraid he was going to come down to my place and find him there. I knew you were a cop,' he said pointing at Joanna. 'I thought if Benji got wind or found out you'd be the first to know.'

'Why didn't you just let him go? No harm, no foul.'

Dean scoffed. 'He saw my face. He knew who I was. You don't fuck with Casey and John Blackwood. They are bad people. I had run out of ideas. I knew I just had to get rid of him. So, I gave him some oxy and morphine, shoved the pills down his throat. That was a bad night.'

'But he didn't die,' Nick replied.

Tears streamed from Dean's eyes and he shook his head. 'No.'

'How did you get to the dam?'

'He was having some sort of a fit, foaming from the mouth. He was yelling, making a heap of noise. I, I just wrapped my hands around his throat until he made no more noise.' The two detectives sat in silence as he continued, 'The dam. It was just the closest thing I could think of. I knew the Smiths were never there. I put him in the back of my ute and drove over there. I tied two concrete blocks to his legs to hold him down. I was pissed and high as a kite. I mustn't have done a very good job.'

***

Nick and Joanna sat with Amelia and Archie in the Inspector's office awaiting the final results of the DNA Troy was testing for them in Dubbo. It was open and shut as far Nick was concerned, the DNA was just the icing on the cake in regard to his actual arrest. They had led the cowboy out of the interrogation room in cuffs, with all pleasantries extinguished after hearing about the young boy's harrowing final few weeks of life.

'We need to speak with John Blackwood,' Nick said to the group. 'I just can't understand why he didn't come to us.'

'He's a pig-headed bastard. Always has been. He probably thought he could deal with it himself,' Archie replied.

'Probably explains why he had an army of his workers out searching day and night for the boy. He'd already received the message. He'd taken it on himself to try and find him. Not get us involved.'

Nick's mind ticked over. He had all the pieces thoroughly in place. Matty's disappearance, Dean being his kidnapper and murderer. Dean's drug use and his ties to Cameron Parsons. Something about the Blackwoods just didn't feel right to him. His mind locked onto a comment Dean had made in the interview and he stood up in the office with a brainwave. 'Give me a sec.'

He walked down to the single cell at the back of the police station. Dean was sitting on the concrete bench. His boots were both off, sitting on the floor with his hat, and he was bent over with his head in his hands. He looked up at Nick's entrance. 'Yeah?'

'You said earlier you knew the Blackwoods were loaded with money due to all of the operations they had going on? What exactly did you mean by that?'

Chapter Forty

Back in the interview room Dean laid out the entire operation. Nick and Joanna sat stunned at what he was describing. He explained that the Blackwoods were a major part of an interstate drug distribution network across Australia. Casey Blackwood's farm had a machinery shed much bigger than any other on the Moroco properties. That storage facility was just off the national highway and was used as a halfway point for many of the biggest drug distributors in the state. Moroco's recent successes had been due to more than luck with weather and crops. The drug distribution supported the farming, and the good years of farming helped further prop up and legitimise their net worth.

The DNA results under Matty's fingernails had come back. They were a 100 percent match. Nick let Joanna do the honours and formally placed Dean under arrest. The job was done on their end, but Nick knew that the real work was only just starting.

'Now we know why he didn't reply to the message,' Nick said to the group.

'Why?' Archie asked.

'We believe he was concerned that any attention on the family would mean attention on their farms, potentially hurting their drug operation,' Joanna added.

Archie was dumbstruck. He seemed unable to comprehend the level of criminality that was right under his nose. Nick had mapped out the story of the Blackwood's given to him by Dean to the Inspector, and now, as the truth was coming to light, more and more things seemed to be falling into place. 'So, what are we going to do?' Archie asked.

Nick was already two steps ahead, and as they all spoke he could see the Chief was calling him. He excused himself into the interview room. 'G'day.'

'How are you?' the Chief asked.

'Good. Dean Taranto has confessed. Laid everything out. Neat as a pin. DNA results came back as a match, Joanna just formally charged him. He took the boy and messaged the kid's grandfather for a ransom.'

'How the hell didn't we know that? Why didn't they tell us?'

Nick grinned. 'This is where things get interesting. Dean is claiming that the Blackwoods have one of the biggest illegal drug distribution storage warehouses in the state. It's a transfer centre. Gear from the cities come out to it, interstate truckers get it and take it where it needs to go. We think that Casey and John Blackwood were concerned that if any heat regarding the disappearance was to come back on them then that they would be found out. That their whole operation would be a bust. That's the going theory anyway.'

'But his own grandson? He'd risk his own grandson's life just for that?'

Nick didn't know what to say. They had both heard of much worse things. 'People are greedy, Chief. Money makes people do terrible things.'

***

Nick and Joanna delivered the news to Gabby Blackwood and Cameron Parsons. Nick was light on the details. Cameron looked like a time bomb ready to explode at any moment. His supposed friend had killed his son and Nick knew, that he knew, it was likely that the drugs he had given Dean had been used for his own son's murder. Nick didn't mention the ransom, and he didn't mention anything about the Blackwood's operation. He kept the details as sparse as he could. Between tears, Gabby kept asking 'why?', but Nick knew they needed the element of surprise, so he just told her that their investigations were still ongoing.

In the end, she thanked them both for their tireless work, particularly Joanna. Nick watched his partner swell with pride at the comments. He knew she deserved it, her hard work and determination was how they'd got this far.

***

It was a two-pronged attack. The Chief had spoken to members of the drug squad about Nick's information and they were mobilised quickly. Apparently there had already been multiple tipoffs to them about drug supply in the area, but they had struggled to pin down any specifics. Two heads of the Drug Squad, along with four special operations members, were helicoptered into Gabinda and were lent a Gabinda Police four-wheel drive. They knew time was of the essence. Nick told them that Dean's arrest had become common knowledge and he was concerned that the Blackwoods could be worried that their operation had been found out.

By the time everyone was organised it was already late afternoon, and the sun was beginning to lower itself in the sky. Nick and Joanna headed down the driveway of Moroco, both content with their arrest and ready to face this final conversation and close out their chapter in Gabinda. Inspector Mick Nash and Senior Sergeant Harry Woodson, from the Drug Squad, sat in the back seat. The Special Operations squad had planned a raid of the storage facility to coincide with the detectives chat, and they advised that if they found what they thought they would, then and only then would they both come inside and arrest John and Casey Blackwood. The Special Operations officers had already assessed the building from the air with their new space-aged drone they had brought along. The building had shown all the signs of being what they thought it was. They were expecting a big find.

There were two utes parked in the driveway and Nick smiled. He could see Casey and John Blackwood up on the deck, along with Casey's wife and child, sitting at the wicker table that overlooked their front lawn. The BBQ beside them had a trail of smoke rising into the clear sky and they both had beers in hand.

'Special Ops are through the gate,' Mick from the Drug Squad said to the two detectives. 'You've got five minutes with them.'

Nick nodded and got out of the car with Joanna. She was dressed more casually than the day before, her usual tied-up hair was out, loosely flowing in the light breeze. He returned her smile. He wasn't sure whether it was just a mental thing or whether it was physical, but she seemed to hold herself differently now, up straighter somehow. She had stepped out on her own as a detective and had more than come to the party. She had delivered in a big way and deserved all the praise she could get.

'What are you smiling at?' she said with a laugh.

Nick shook his head. 'Nothing. Just you. You've done a bloody great job, mate. This is all your hard work right here.'

'Thank you,' she replied. 'I couldn't have done it without you.'

Nick opened the small wire gate and allowed Joanna to go ahead. The group all stayed seated but were looking at the two detectives as they walked over the front lawn. Nick stepped up onto the deck first. 'Nice night for it,' Nick said.

John sipped from his beer. 'It is. How can we help you, detectives?'

Nick stepped up to the table and slid a chair out for Joanna. 'Do you mind if we take a seat?'

'Of course,' John replied.

Nick sat down and inspected the group. He could tell Casey and his wife were nervous. Their usual laidback demeanour was absent. Nick wondered whether they suspected how much he knew. He was about to find out.

'So, as you all know by now, Dean Taranto has been arrested for Matty's kidnap and murder. We let Gabby and Cameron know this morning.'

'She was here just before,' Casey said. 'Thank you for giving us answers. We appreciate it more than you will ever know.'

'You're welcome.' He looked at the group. 'There are just a few loose ends we wanted to tie up, now this is all done.'

'Oh yeah?' John asked.

'Yeah,' Nick replied. 'When Dean Taranto admitted to the murder, he told us everything. He told us about the pills. How he gets them from Cameron Parsons and where Cameron gets them from.'

'Cameron doesn't know shit,' Casey replied.

Nick was bluffing but praying the special operations team found what they needed. 'That's where you're wrong. Your brother-in-law knew a fair bit more than you realise about your little operation out on Riverleigh next to the main highway.' Casey stiffened and looked at his father. John sipped from his beer again and leaned back in his chair. Nick felt zero pity for the millionaire landowner. He had chosen his own financial gain over the life of his grandson. John made him sick. He waited to see if Casey was going to reply and then prepared to drop the bombshell. 'And we also know *why* Matty was killed. We know why Dean did it,' he added.

'Why?' Casey asked. 'The boy didn't deserve to die.'

Nick turned to John and pulled out the leather-bound note pad he usually carried for interviews. He opened it and pulled out phone records he'd got that morning from Hattie. 'Phone records from Dean Taranto's phone show he text messaged your father a total of six times. One the morning after Matty's disappearance, and sporadically again over the next few weeks. Those text messages were ransom requests. Requests for your father to pony up one million dollars for Matty's return.'

As Nick spoke, John placed his beer down and put his head in his hands. Casey's mouth was open in shock. He didn't look like he could compute what Nick was saying and turned to his father. 'Dad. What the hell is he saying? Is that true?'

John lifted his face up out of his hands. His calm demeanour was gone. The police knew. And now his son knew. He sighed and looked at Casey. 'I didn't know what to do, mate. I knew if I had told the cops they would have overrun the place. You know I didn't want to risk what we've got going on.'

Casey slid back in his chair as his face turned a bright shade of red. Nick turned to see the two drug squad detectives walking across the lawn. One of them gave him a subtle nod which told Nick everything. They had found what they needed.

'Are you serious right now?' Casey pointed at his father. You fuckin' killed him! This is all your fault! You were too fuckin' greedy! I told you!'

John stood up. 'Please, Casey, just let me explain.'

'You can talk in your cells,' Joanna said, pointing to the two officers behind them. 'These men here from the Drug Squad would like to speak with you.'

Chapter Forty-One

John and Casey Blackwood were both arrested on the spot. The Special Operations team members had found one of the biggest drug distribution warehouses they had ever seen. They were both going to go to prison for a long time, and it was more than a worthy punishment for John, Nick thought, to sit in a cell and think about that one greedy decision he had made, for the rest of his life.

Dean Taranto was transferred to Sydney for holding before his trial. Nick and Joanna both testified during his arrest hearing. The case was open and shut, there wasn't any more evidence required for convicting someone of committing murder. Dean Taranto sobbed in the stands like a broken man when the verdict was read out. Guilty on all charges. He was going to spend the rest of his life in prison. Nick wondered if he had asked the cowboy one year ago how the rest of his life was going to turn out, whether he could have even imagined that he'd be spending it behind bars. It was no happy ending for a man of the land, but it was a life he now more than deserved.

***

Now that Nick and Joanna were back in Sydney, Joanna finally got a chance to take some proper time off. Glenn arrived a week later, content to leave the rodeo behind forever, and they spent a few sleepless nights in her apartment really getting to know each other. She was happier now than she ever had been before. To be wanted by a man and to have someone else to rely on was a welcome change. She told him she wanted to take things slowly and he told her he had all the time in the world. She loved that about him - his patience - it was something her enigmatic crime fighting partner could use a little of from time to time.

Nick threw himself back into rehab. Physically, he was okay. He joined a local gym near his house and was trying to stay consistent, and he started running even more regularly. Mentally, it was a different story. His therapist gave him different memory exercises to work on but he knew he wasn't quite there yet. She told him that it would all take time and he needed to be patient.

The Chief had started to load his in-tray up with new cases and he cautiously returned to his city office to start reading through some. Joanna returned after her break and together they began to split files and dig deep, but nothing in the files screamed out for them to hit the road again. None of them looked ready to make any progress.

Joanna placed a file down on the bench one day and sighed. Nothing about the case they were looking into, the three-year-old murder of a father of five seemed to jump out at them. 'You still on for tonight?'

Nick smiled. 'I wouldn't miss it.'

***

That night, they both stood behind the stands of the massive arena. It was the first round of the Wrangler Pro Bull Riding Championship in Sydney. The round rodeo fencing had been erected on the pristine grass and the crowd roared in anticipation of the night's festivities. Nick watched the group of cowboys beside the trailer. The elderly man in the centre was giving them a rousing speech. This was their moment, this was where the real pressure was, this was their time to shine, he said to them. Nick felt the energy in the group and grinned at the man; he felt like jumping on a bull himself in that moment.

The riders broke away to start grabbing their gear, and Neville Ford walked over to them with Benji by his side. He wrapped Joanna up in a rough hug and then shook Nick's hand. 'I'm bloody sorry we didn't get a chance to chat after everything went down,' he said. 'I just wanted to say how sorry I am for being a part of all this. If I hadda' known, you know I would've said something.'

'Nothing you could have done,' Nick said. 'We're just glad we caught him.'

Neville shook his head. 'I still can't bloody believe it. I thought he was a mate. And the Blackwoods.' He grimaced. 'I always knew something was up with that lot.'

'You seen Gabby around?' Joanna asked.

'Sure,' Neville replied. 'She's moved into Moroco with Cameron. They are gonna try and make a go of it.' He laughed. 'Cameron knows as much about farming as my old boot though, unfortunately.'

***

Nick sat in the stands with Joanna and Glenn, looking forward to the show. It was Benji's debut ride on the pro circuit. His pre-season had been great, Joanna had said, and this was the main reason why Neville chose him to represent his team at this prestigious event.

'Next up is Benji Gray out of Gabinda, riding for Neville Ford's squad,' yelled the announcer. 'He's pulled the short straw tonight and will be riding a fan favourite.' A drumroll came over the speakers. 'Everyone, give it up for Bandsaw!'

The crowd cheered and Nick saw Joanna's face go grey.

'Shit, That was the bull that nearly killed Bryce,' Glenn said to him.

Joanna slapped Glenn on the leg. 'You didn't need to say it. Jesus, I need a wine.' She picked up Nick and Glenn's hands each side of her in unison. 'Pray for him, please.'

The crowd fell silent as Benji hovered over the giant bull. It was a ghostly black and it shunted aggressively back and forward. Nick could hear the clanging and crashing from high up in the stands. 'Pull!' was yelled and the gate exploded open.

The bull flew outward at a million miles an hour while the announcer roared. Benji held on for dear life as it launched into the air, to Joanna's cheers and screams. As it landed, it suddenly kicked violently to the left, and Benji, fully prepared for the twist, expertly adjusted his body to the rhythm of the enormous beast. The crowd screamed in unison as the ride reached its crescendo and he threw his left leg over the beast and landed down on his two feet, facing the crowd. He tipped his hat to their cheers and gave them a theatrical bow.

'Benji Gray!' the announcer yelled. 'Fifteen seconds on one of the hardest bulls in the nation! I think this young fella is well on his way to super stardom!'

Joanna was still squeezing Nick's hand. 'Jesus, I can't feel my fingers,' he said with a laugh.

Joanna hit both their thighs. She had tears on her face and was crying with Joy. 'He did it! GO BENJI!' she yelled.

Nick felt his phone vibrate in his pocket and he pulled it out. He had four missed calls from the Chief. He showed Joanna the phone. 'Shit, I need to call him.'

He raced down the steep stairs in the bleachers and went down the concrete tunnel towards the riders' area where it was quiet. He flashed his all-access pass to the security guard and continued on out into the car park. He dialled the Chief's number and Mark answered on the second ring. 'Hey Chief, what's up?'

'Shit Nick. I've been calling you for an hour.'

'Yeah sorry, I'm at the rodeo with Joanna,' Nick replied.

'Well, pack your bags, mate. There's been a murder in Milford.'

Jason Summers

THE END

The Lost Boy

Thank you so much for reading my novel.

If you enjoyed *The Lost Boy*, make sure you check out the rest of the Detective Nick Vada Series:

Warranilla

Into The Flames

The Storm

The Kooleybuc Hotel

The Last Sunset

Murder In Secret

The Thief

The Devil In The Sky

The Lost Boy

They are all on Amazon Books now.

Also, if you enjoyed my novel, please consider leaving a rating and review on my Amazon book page or on Goodreads. It means a lot to hear what my readers think as reviews are hard to come by and I personally read every review.

Jason Summers

Printed in Dunstable, United Kingdom

66078188R00190